Lorcan knows Devon is his mate. What he doesn't know is what to do with that. If it had been anyone else, he would have talked to them, but Devon is on the run from his abusive ex, a man who is planning to attack Gillham and the pack, and Lorcan doesn't want to spook Devon more than he already is.

Devon never wants to see his ex again. He hates the man, even though they're mates—or are they? That's what Elroy said, but as time passes and he finds himself drawn to Lorcan, Devon starts to wonder.

Lorcan and Devon know they have a lot of work to do if they want to be together. Devon needs to understand that Lorcan isn't going to hurt him and that he's nothing like Elroy, but he's not sure he can. Then there's Elroy, who's still in the background, threatening Devon.

Devon wants a future with Lorcan, but is it too much to hope for? Elroy won't let go of him easily, and neither will fear. He'll have to fight both of them to get the life he wants. The only problem is that he's not sure he's strong enough.

Lorcan
Copyright © 2020 Catherine Lievens
ISBN: 978-1-4874-2927-0
Cover art by Angela Waters

Published by eXtasy Books Inc or
Devine Destinies, an imprint of eXtasy Books Inc

Look for us online at:
www.eXtasybooks.com or www.devinedestinies.com

LORCAN
COUNCIL ENFORCERS BOOK 23

BY

CATHERINE LIEVENS

CHAPTER ONE

Devon was Lorcan's mate. That was the only thing Lorcan knew for sure right now.

He had no idea what to do about it, either. He'd sat in the meeting where Devon had explained what his ex-boyfriend — if the man could even be called that — had done to him. He'd been terrified, and Lorcan doubted that would change anytime soon. That meant he had to stay away from Devon, no matter how much he wanted to rush to him and tell him what they were to each other. The last thing he wanted was to scare Devon even more, and no matter how much it hurt not to do it, he knew it was the best thing he could do for Devon.

"Okay. Something is going on, and we need to know what it is," Jonathan said as he sat on the couch opposite Lorcan.

Lorcan blinked at him. He hadn't even heard Jonathan and Tanner come in, which made him a lousy enforcer. Of course, he was in the enforcers' building, so he knew he was safe. Still, he should have known. "I don't know what you're talking about," he tried.

Tanner rolled his eyes. "Sure you don't. That's why you've been moping around for the past few weeks." His teasing smile dropped. "But you know you can talk to us, right? I mean, we're team members, but we're also friends. Or at least, I'd like to think we are."

Lorcan shook himself. He didn't want his friends to think he didn't care about them or that he didn't trust them. "Of course we're friends."

Tanner nodded. "Good. Tell us, then."

Lorcan hesitated. He didn't want to say anything about Devon, just in case Devon wouldn't want anyone to know. Hell, considering how frightened Devon was, he probably didn't.

But Lorcan also needed to talk to someone. He needed a sounding board, someone to tell him what to do. Right now, the only thing he'd managed to decide was that he needed to stay away from Devon, but it was becoming harder and harder. Devon hadn't rejected him, and Lorcan felt the bond between them keenly. It made him and his eagle want to go to their mate, want to push through the pain and fear to get Devon to *see*, but he doubted it would help. If anything, it would probably scare Devon even more, and that was the last thing Lorcan wanted. He never wanted his mate to be afraid of him.

"Lorcan?" Jonathan asked. There was so much doubt in his voice, as if he wasn't sure what was happening and not knowing hurt him. It probably did. They were friends, even though they'd begun as team members.

Lorcan sighed. "Okay. I'll tell you. But you can't tell anyone."

"Do we look like we're going to gossip? You know we won't tell anyone. It's your thing to confess, both to us and to anyone else."

"And you can't do anything about it, either."

Jonathan blinked. "What would we want to do about it? We don't even know what *it* is."

"Not yet, but you will soon. You're here because you want to find out, aren't you?"

"Only if it makes you feel better. We're worried about you, Lorcan. You haven't been yourself the past few weeks, and while we gave you space until now, we're starting to think that it's not what you need."

It *wasn't* what Lorcan needed. What Lorcan needed was his

mate, but he knew he wouldn't get him.

He sucked in a breath. "I met my mate," he finally said. He might as well just say the words and see what happened.

There was a pause, then Tanner asked, "I take it that it wasn't a happy meeting?"

Lorcan shook his head. "It's Devon."

"Shit. You mean the Devon who came here to talk to Kameron? The one who's dating the guy who wants to destroy Gillham?"

"*Was* dating," Lorcan snapped. He gave Tanner an apologetic glance. "Sorry. But he *was* dating Elroy. He's not anymore."

"Because he was an abusive dick. We know. We were there when he talked to Kameron." Tanner bit his lower lip, which was an odd gesture for such a big man. "I don't know if I should congratulate you or if I should feel sorry for you," he admitted.

Tanner was human, so he couldn't fully understand how bad Lorcan felt about all this. He'd been around shifters long enough to know what Lorcan was talking about, but still. He'd never gone through it, and he never would.

"Does he know?" Jonathan asked.

Lorcan shook his head. "I haven't told him. You saw him. You *heard* him. He's terrified, and I didn't want to make it worse."

Jonathan slowly nodded.

Lorcan could tell he was turning over what Lorcan had told him in his mind, trying to find a solution. There probably wasn't one.

"Shouldn't you tell him?" Tanner asked.

"I should, but he's terrified. What do you think he's going to think if a shifter he doesn't know tells him he's his mate? After what Elroy put him through, I doubt he trusts anyone, let alone guys who want to get in his pants."

Jonathan barked out a laugh. "That's not the only thing you want to do, though. I mean, yes, you're attracted to him, and I can see why. He's cute. But more importantly, he's your mate." He paused and cocked his head. "Unless you do only want to get in his pants?"

Lorcan glared at him. "Of course not. What would you want if you met your mate? Just to have sex with him?" Lorcan shook his head. "I want *everything* with him. I know it's ridiculous because we haven't even talked, but I've been thinking about him nonstop for the past few weeks, and I'm getting desperate. I want to at least talk to him."

"Then do it. Talk to him."

"He doesn't even leave the house," Lorcan pointed out. Devon lived with Justin, one of their team members, and Justin's mate. He'd been living there when Justin had bought the derelict house. Devon had been homeless, and the house had been the only place he felt safe. Lorcan was grateful to Justin and his mate, who had welcomed him in their life and hadn't forced him to move out when they bought the house. A lot of people would have, and it would have put Devon back on the streets. Instead, he had a home and two friends. That was what he needed, but Lorcan couldn't help but wonder if it also was what he *wanted*.

He shook his head at his thoughts. He was projecting what he wanted onto Devon, and he couldn't. Devon didn't know they were mates. He didn't want Lorcan the way Lorcan wanted him.

Jonathan leaned closer. "We're not going to force you to do anything,"

Lorcan startled. "You can try."

Jonathan rolled his eyes. "As I was saying, we're not going to force you to do anything. We can't, and we don't want to. I think I'm talking for both of us when I say we hope you'll eventually tell Devon about this, and that he'll be happy to find out. We know how bad things can be, though, and we'll be here for you if you need anything. But talk to him, Lorcan. He deserves to know, even if he rejects you. I know it's hard to wrap your mind around the fact that he could, but you need to think about it. He still deserves to know that you're his mate, though. It's a bond he won't find anywhere else, and if he has a chance at a good relationship with you and at happiness, he should know about it."

Lorcan agreed. Of course he did. The only reason he knew he and Devon were mates was that he was a shifter, while Devon was human and couldn't feel their bond. That didn't mean he didn't deserve to know. It was as important to Devon as it was to Lorcan, even though he couldn't feel it.

How was Lorcan supposed to tell him, though? Could he just go up to Justin's front door, knock, and tell him that he needed to see Devon because they were mates?

He didn't know. That was why he'd been thinking about it for the past few weeks, and he still didn't have an answer.

At this point, he doubted he would ever find one.

Devon could hear Justin and Yedley in the living room, and the sound of their conversation made his heart hurt. They were mates, and they were bonded. They were each other's future, and they would never hurt each other.

Elroy had hurt him, though. Being mates hadn't mattered. He'd never claimed Devon, and Devon suspected he'd never planned to. He probably didn't want to because Devon was a human, and Devon was grateful he'd managed to get out of that relationship. He was grateful now that Elroy had never claimed him. He would have been stuck with him—abused and broken.

Now, though, he was free, or at least, as free as he could be. It didn't matter to him that he never left the house. He didn't want to, not when leaving might mean that Elroy could find him. *No.* He was much safer inside, and the only way he would ever leave was if Justin or Yedley kicked him out.

He hoped they wouldn't.

When they'd bought the house, he'd thought he would lose it. He'd been living there even though there hadn't been electricity or running water—even though it had been a mess and bitterly cold. It was the only place he'd felt safe after running away from Elroy, though, and it still was. Of course, these days, the house looked better. Justin and Yedley had been working on it, as had Devon, and most of the rooms were livable. There were still a few issues, but nothing like it had been when Devon had first lived here.

He was lucky Justin and Yedley hadn't kicked him out. It would have been within their rights, especially after they bought the house. He'd been squatting and terrified of both them and everyone else in town.

He was still terrified of Elroy.

He hadn't always been like this. He'd been a normal person before he'd met Elroy. Then, everything had gone up in flames. Elroy had told him they were mates, that they belonged together, and Devon had been stupid enough to believe him. But now, he knew that being mates didn't always mean your mate loved you. It wasn't always like the relationship Justin and Yedley shared. They truly were happy together, and Devon couldn't help but feel slightly jealous. He'd never have that. He'd run away from his mate, and he was never going back.

Of course, Elroy could always find him. He didn't know Devon was in Gillham, and Devon hoped he would never find out. Still, it was a possibility he couldn't ignore.

What if Elroy realized where he was? What if he knew Devon had come here to warn the pack, and he attacked them before they were ready to defend themselves?

Devon shook his head. He couldn't think that way. He had to stop thinking about this stuff because there was nothing more he could do. He'd reached Gillham and told the people in charge what Elroy was planning. Everything else was out of his control. He couldn't stop Elroy, just like he hadn't been able to stop him when he'd abused him.

He sighed and pushed one of the mushrooms in the pan too hard, sending it flying.

It wasn't that he didn't like his life. He realized he'd been lucky. A lot of people weren't able to run from their abuser. A lot of people didn't try, and he understood why. He'd spent much more time with Elroy than he should have, especially considering how Elroy had treated him.

But he'd managed to get out. He'd left, and now he was free, even though he was stuck in a house that wasn't his. He had friends, and he had a hard time believing it. He couldn't deny it, though. Why else would Justin and Yedley have allowed him to stay, even though they knew Elroy was after him?

Because Devon was sure that eventually, Elroy would find him. The man had always been like a dog with a bone when he wanted something. That was one of the reasons Devon had given in to him in the first place. When they'd first met, he'd been fascinated, but he'd also been able to tell there was something off with Elroy. He'd brushed it off, telling himself that it was only because Elroy was a shifter and he wasn't, so he didn't fully understand what it meant.

But it wasn't that. Devon should have listened to his instincts, but he hadn't, and he'd ended up being abused. He'd been beaten and demeaned, and the thought of going back was terrifying. He knew what Elroy would do to him if he managed to get his hands on him again, and he would do everything he could to make sure that didn't happen.

He wasn't sure it would be enough, though.

7

"You don't have to do that," a voice said from behind Devon, and he startled so hard that the wooden spoon he'd been using to stir the food flew from his hand.

To his surprise, Justin managed to snatch it before it hit the floor. "Here you go," he said, handing it back to Devon.

Devon forced himself to smile at him. He wanted to smile at Justin, who was helping him more than anyone else in the world ever had, but he never *felt* like smiling anymore. "Thank you," he murmured.

Justin nodded and leaned back against the counter, crossing his arms over his chest. "You don't have to do that," he repeated.

Devon shrugged. "I want to." Actually, he didn't enjoy cooking — the only reason he was doing it was that he felt he owed it to Justin and Yedley.

They didn't have to welcome him into their home. They didn't have to give him a bedroom, to protect him the way they were, to make him a part of their family. Hell, the two of them had just met and bonded. As far as Devon knew, they should have wanted him out so they could spend time alone together. They never said anything about it, though, and Devon knew they wouldn't. They wanted him to feel safe, and he did.

He also felt like a dead weight.

He wanted to do more. He wished he could, but leaving the house was out of the question for him. He couldn't risk it. He couldn't risk someone seeing him and recognizing him, telling Elroy where he was. He had no doubt Elroy had people in Gillham. He was planning on attacking the town and taking over the pack, and he wouldn't do that haphazardly. He was a planner, which meant he'd probably sent some of his men here to look around and spy on the pack.

Devon couldn't risk leaving the house. That meant he couldn't find a job, couldn't go grocery shopping, couldn't do much to help Yedley and Justin. Cooking was something he *could* do, no matter how much he disliked it, so that was what he did.

Justin sighed, and Devon took a step back. He didn't want to displease his friend. He didn't want to displease anyone.

"You can cook if you want, of course," Justin said. "I know you don't like it, though."

Devon shrugged and tried to stop his heart from racing. Justin wouldn't hurt him. He wasn't that kind of man. He wasn't the kind of man Elroy was.

"I don't mind," Devon murmured.

"I know you don't. I just—don't do stuff you don't like."

"This is the only thing I can do."

Justin raked a hand through his hair. "That's what I was trying to say. You don't *have* to do anything. Yedley and I didn't agree to have you live with us so you could cook for us. We want you to have a safe place, a place where you can be yourself. Being yourself isn't forcing yourself to cook even though you hate it."

Devon plastered a smile on his face and turned to look at Justin. "Well, I would have to force myself to cook even if I lived alone, wouldn't I? I have to eat. So do you. What does it matter that I'm the one cooking?"

Justin still looked frustrated, and Devon was sorry. He wanted to make Justin and Yedley's life easy, but he was making a mess out of it.

Justin patted Devon's shoulder. "Fine. Cook if you want to. I just want you to know you don't have to, especially when we're having people over for dinner."

"I know." That much, Devon was sure of. Justin and Yedley didn't expect anything from him, even though it felt wrong. This was the least he could do for them, even though Justin insisted he didn't have to. It was a way to feel okay with himself and the situation, so he wouldn't stop.

He couldn't.

Lorcan was nervous. He shouldn't be. Justin and Yedley had invited him and the rest of the team for dinner. Devon had nothing to do with it. He would only be there because he lived there, too, but that didn't mean he *wanted* Lorcan there.

A pang of pain squeezed Lorcan's chest. Of course Devon wouldn't want him there. Why would he? He didn't trust anyone but Justin and Yedley, and that hurt. Lorcan realized it was neither his nor Devon's fault. After everything Devon had gone through, it was normal for him not to trust people. He couldn't feel the bond as keenly as Lorcan did, and that meant he wasn't as influenced by it as Lorcan.

He wouldn't trust Lorcan just because they were mates. It would take more than that, but Lorcan would have to talk to him to start that process. Instead, he'd chickened out for two weeks, and now, he was about to see Devon again, and he was both nervous and elated. He wanted to see Devon. He wanted to talk to him, to ask him how he was, to make sure he was okay. He didn't know if he would be able to do any of that, though.

"Are you sure you're okay?" Jonathan asked. He sounded worried, which was probably because Lorcan had been all over the place since their conversation. He shouldn't have talked to him and Tanner about this, not today, not right before the three of them had to leave to go to Justin's house.

Lorcan supposed he should be lucky the rest of the team wasn't coming. They all had something to do, so it would be just the three of them, Justin, Yedley, and Devon. Only six people, and Lorcan was freaking out.

He forced himself to nod. "I'm fine," he said.

"Tanner and I suggested you talk to him, but you don't have to do it now."

"I know."

Lorcan wasn't planning on talking to Devon tonight. He didn't think he'd be able to. The last thing he wanted was to scare Devon off, and a nice friendly dinner wasn't the best occasion to tell him they were mates. Of course, Lorcan doubted there would ever be a perfect occasion. Devon would freak out no matter what he said or when he said it. Lorcan couldn't seem to force himself to say the words for that reason. He didn't blame Devon, knowing what he did of Devon's past, but it didn't help him accept it.

When they arrived at Justin's house, Lorcan's hands were sweaty. He rubbed his palms on his thighs, plastered a smile on his face, and stood behind Jonathan and Tanner as they waited.

The door opened, and Yedley smiled at them. "Hello," he said, stepping to the side.

The house smelled good, and Lorcan's stomach grumbled. Yedley heard it and smiled at him, then winked. "Don't worry. We'll feed you soon."

"What's for dinner?" Tanner asked.

"Devon's cooking a stir fry. I hope that's okay with you. We didn't want to do anything too complicated, especially since there are six of us and he insisted on cooking."

"It's perfect," Lorcan said. There was probably something in his tone, because Yedley looked at him quizzically. Lorcan forced himself to smile. "I mean, it's not easy to go from cooking for three to cooking for six, especially when, well, you know. I mean, he doesn't like to cook, right?" Justin had mentioned it, and Lorcan had memorized it the way he memorized anything that had to do with Devon.

Yedley slowly nodded. "I do know." His smile widened. "But we got a cake from a bakery, so save some space for dessert."

Lorcan didn't know if Yedley suspected something, but he

11

hoped not. He wanted to be the one to tell Devon about this. He didn't know if Yedley would if he found out, but he didn't want to risk it, just in case.

He, Jonathan, and Tanner stepped into the house. It did smell good, and Lorcan didn't care that it was a stir fry. Hell, he loved stir fry. It was simple yet filling, and from the smell of it, this one was going to be good.

"You know where the living room is," Yedley said. "Justin is in the kitchen, though, so if you want to go there, we can have a chat."

Tanner and Jonathan followed Yedley to the kitchen, but Lorcan hung back. Devon was in there. He was the one cooking, so he would be at the stove. Lorcan didn't want to scare him, though, so he decided to stay away. It was going to be a bit awkward if he was the only one in the living room, though. He wasn't sure there was anything he could do about it, so instead of being there alone, he hovered at the kitchen door, looking in.

He was right. Devon *was* at the stove, and he was carefully avoiding looking around the room. He'd waved at Tanner and Jonathan when they walked in, but he hadn't looked at them.

Since he wasn't looking at Lorcan, either, Lorcan took a moment to look at him.

He was gorgeous. His blond hair fell in front of his eyes, and he had to push it away periodically. It hindered his ability to see, but Lorcan doubted he would do anything about it, not when he couldn't leave the house. It didn't make him any less gorgeous.

He was thin, still *too* thin, and that thought made Lorcan want to hit something, or rather, someone. If he ever got his hands on Elroy, he would make sure the man knew what he thought about him, and he would make sure to tell him with his fists.

Devon appeared more relaxed than he'd been the last time Lorcan saw him. That was probably because that last time had been during a meeting with Kameron. Devon had talked about his ex-boyfriend, about what the man was planning for Gillham, and he'd been terrified. He hadn't been afraid just of Elroy, but also of Kameron. He hadn't known Kameron, and he hadn't realized he could trust the alpha. Lorcan didn't blame him, even though he'd known Kameron for years.

"Why are you over there?" Justin asked suddenly.

Lorcan blinked. It took him a second to realize Justin was talking to him, and when he did, he shrugged and rubbed the back of his neck. "No reason."

"Why don't you come in? We'll have dinner soon, so you should probably sit at the table with us. Unless you want to eat there?"

Lorcan felt his cheeks heat. He prayed he wasn't blushing as he stepped more fully into the kitchen. Justin arched a brow, clearly puzzled by Lorcan's behavior, and Lorcan couldn't blame him. They were friends, yet he hadn't told Justin about this. He wasn't planning to, either. Justin was one of Devon's closest friends, and Lorcan didn't want that to change. He knew that admitting they were mates would change things. It didn't matter that Justin was both his and Devon's friend. He wanted Devon to have Justin on his side.

Justin would never do anything to hurt Devon. He *would* be on Devon's side, always, even if it meant going against Lorcan. Lorcan didn't want him to have to choose, though.

He took a step back, moving into the hallway again. "I have to go to the bathroom." He was running, but he needed a moment.

He took his time in the bathroom, washing his face as well as his hands. He needed a minute to gather his thoughts, to make sure he could go back to the kitchen without anyone guessing what was going on in his brain.

He should have known better. When he opened the bathroom door, Justin was standing there, leaning against the wall, looking at him. Lorcan forced himself to smile. "Bathroom's free."

Justin nodded, but he didn't move. "What's going on with you?" he asked instead.

Lorcan huffed. "Why are you all asking that? I'm fine."

"Jonathan and Tanner got to you, huh?"

Lorcan nodded. "Of course they did. You know them."

"I do, and I know you. I can tell something is going on."

Lorcan was tempted to brush him off, but he knew better than to do that. He knew better than to try to brush off any of his team members. If they worried too much, they would go to their team leader, and she would put Lorcan on the sidelines until she was sure he was okay. Lorcan couldn't allow that to happen, not when Elroy might attack Gillham at any moment.

"Are you and Devon mates?" Justin asked.

Lorcan blinked at him. He didn't think he could have gotten a word out of his mouth even if he'd tried, so he took a moment to think about what Justin had just said.

Justin knew, and Lorcan had no idea how. Was it obvious? How could it be, since he and Devon never spent time together? He cleared his throat. Once again, he thought about lying to Justin and tell him everything was okay and that he was wrong. They were in the same team, though, and more importantly, they were friends. They trusted each other, and that couldn't change.

He looked away. "We are," he quietly admitted.

Justin nodded. "I suspected for a while."

Lorcan snorted. "How? I didn't tell anyone until today, and the only reason I admitted it to Jonathan and Tanner was that they pushed."

"I don't know. I think I noticed something when you and

the others came to help us with the house that day. Then I kept an eye on you and Devon when we took him to talk to Kameron. I didn't know for sure until you told me, though."

The only person who'd known for sure until today was Lorcan, and he was making a mess of things. He rubbed the back of his neck. "I don't know what to do about it," he confessed. "He's scared. His ex is after him, and I don't want him to see me as a threat."

"I don't think he does."

"What do you think I should do?" Justin knew Devon better than anyone. He certainly knew him better than Lorcan did. Maybe he would have an answer.

Justin took a moment before saying, "I think we should talk to him," he eventually said. "You should probably do it here. He feels safe in the house, and he knows we're around. It might help."

There was nothing Lorcan wanted less than that. He did want to tell Devon they were mates, but he doubted today was the right moment, or that Justin's house was the right place. Still, it was what Justin thought he should do, and Justin and Devon were friends. Maybe he wasn't wrong. Maybe Lorcan needed to take that step.

Lorcan didn't think he could.

Devon was an idiot. He needed to stay away from men, not notice them. He wasn't in the market for a relationship, and he doubted he ever would be.

Why couldn't he help but notice Lorcan, then?

Justin wouldn't be friends with someone as bad as Elroy. Hell, Justin wouldn't be friends with anyone who was an asshole. That meant Lorcan was probably safe, or as safe as any person could be. Still, that didn't mean Devon needed to think about him as a possible boyfriend.

15

He couldn't help it, though. Something inside him warmed when he was with Lorcan, and he couldn't explain it. He felt like he needed to talk to the man, to find out more about him. Did Lorcan have a boyfriend? A girlfriend? When had he become an enforcer? Did he find Devon attractive?

Devon's cheeks heated, and he focused on the food he was plating. He had to stop thinking about that. Even if he was in the mood for a relationship—which he definitely wasn't—why would Lorcan want him? He was an idiot. He'd stayed with an abusive man even though he'd been hurt. Who would want to be with him when he couldn't even take care of himself, let alone someone else? Certainly not Lorcan.

Lorcan was an enforcer, which meant he was smart. He deserved to be with someone just as smart as him. Hell, he could probably have anyone he wanted. He was a gorgeous man, with dark curls and dark eyes. He made Devon want to curl against him, and it took everything Devon had to stay away from him.

It was hard, though. Lorcan wasn't just gorgeous. He was also quite adorable, especially in the way he treated Devon. Devon had caught him staring a few times, and every single time, Lorcan looked away and blushed. It was like he wanted to talk to Devon, to be close to him, but Devon had a hard time believing that.

Lorcan probably had questions about Devon's past. He might want to know if Devon had heard about Elroy again, if he knew anything more than he had when he'd talked to Alpha Rhett. Devon had to convince himself of that before he did something stupid.

He didn't understand why he felt the way he did. He didn't have an explanation for it. He tried to ignore it during dinner, but it was hard. It was so hard that Yedley noticed something, and once they were in the kitchen alone again after dinner, he moved closer.

"Is everything okay?" he asked.

Devon nodded. "Of course."

"You've been quiet." Yedley softly snorted. "I mean, you've been quieter than usual."

"I'm sorry," Devon murmured.

Yedley shook his head and squeezed Devon's arm. "It's not a bad thing. I don't expect you to have long conversations with me. I'm starting to get to know you, and I know it's not your thing. But I'm worried. Should we not have asked our friends to come over for dinner? Is that what makes you uncomfortable?"

Devon shook his head, then nodded. It made Yedley laugh, and Devon couldn't help but smile. "Okay, so maybe their presence makes me nervous. It doesn't mean you have to kick them out, though."

"I wouldn't say we're planning on kicking them out. But I'm sure that if we explained the problem, they'd understand."

"I don't want you to have to give this up because I'm around. They're your friends. You're allowed to ask them over for dinner, and they're allowed to be here and to enjoy it."

"But you're my friend, too. If what you need is to be left alone, we'll ask the others to leave."

Devon shook his head. "I know they won't hurt me. You wouldn't be friends with them if they would." He hesitated. Yedley probably didn't have an answer for him, but maybe he would have an idea of why Devon felt the way he did when it came to Lorcan. Devon was only human. Yedley might not be a shifter, but he was a Nix. "I just feel weird when Lorcan is around," he admitted.

Yedley cocked his head. "Can you elaborate? Weird can mean a lot of things."

"I'm not sure myself. I feel I should talk to him. My

stomach flutters, and I want to be close to him. I know it doesn't make sense since I don't know him. Do you think there's something there? I mean, why do you think I feel this way?"

Yedley bit his lower lip. Devon could tell from his expression that he probably wouldn't like what he was about to say, but he needed to know, so he waited, holding his breath.

"Have you thought about the fact that Lorcan might be your mate?" Yedley eventually asked.

Devon snorted so loudly he was pretty sure Justin heard him from the living room. "That's not possible," he said.

Yedley cocked a brow. "It's not?"

"Of course not. Humans only have one mate, right?"

"Well, I think it's more complicated than that. Some of the people who live with the pack have a second mate."

Devon had never heard of that, and he had a lot of questions. "Is their first mate still around, though?"

"No. Gentry's mate died some time ago." Yedley blinked. "Are you telling me you have a mate?"

"I do, and he's still alive."

"Do you want to talk about it?"

Devon never wanted to talk about Elroy, but Yedley deserved an explanation. "It's one of the reasons I stayed with Elroy as long as I did. We were mates."

Yedley looked at Devon for so long that Devon started to wonder what was going on, then, he asked, "Are you sure you were mates?"

Devon shrugged. "I can't exactly tell, can I? I'm human. But he told me we were mates, and since he's a shifter, it has to be the truth."

"Some shifters lie, you know. Maybe he was lying to you because he wanted to keep you around."

Devon's heart felt like it stopped in his chest. He'd been clinging to the knowledge of being Elroy's mate for so long.

He couldn't believe he was considering the fact it might have been a lie. "You think he lied to me," he said.

"I think it would have been convenient for him to lie, yes. He wanted to keep you around, and the fact that supposedly you're his mate made that happen. You might have left sooner if you hadn't believed it."

Devon couldn't deny that. He'd been thinking the same thing a few minutes earlier. "Still. How am I supposed to know if he was lying?"

"You just told me you felt drawn to Lorcan."

"I do."

Yedley nodded. "Feeling drawn to someone is a sign they might be your mate. It's harder with humans, since they don't feel the bond as strongly as shifters do, but it might be an explanation."

Devon's world was flipped once again. He didn't know if it was a good or a bad thing, though. It could start a new part of Devon's life if he allowed it.

Everything was too complicated, though. He couldn't think about this right now, yet he also couldn't stop thinking about it. "What should I do?" he asked, his voice barely a louder than a whisper.

"Talk to him. He's the only one who can confirm whether or not you're mates. I know you don't trust him or anyone, really, but I promise you, Lorcan is a good person. He won't force you into anything. None of our friends will."

Devon knew he was right. He trusted Justin and Yedley, and if they trusted their friends, then so should Devon. It didn't make it easier. He couldn't imagine himself having this kind of conversation with Lorcan or with anyone. Still, if Elroy had lied to him, he wanted to know. He needed to know.

CHAPTER TWO

Lorcan didn't mind being sent out on missions with the enforcers' team, but for once, he was glad they weren't going anywhere. Bran and Kameron wanted all the enforcers in Gillham just in case Elroy did something, and it was more than okay with Lorcan. He wanted to be close to Devon if Devon needed him, even though Devon had no idea they were mates. It wasn't just that, though. Lorcan's parents and his family lived in Gillham, and he needed to be able to protect them in case something happened.

He'd been worried since he'd found out what Elroy was planning. He hated having to wait and not being able to find out what was going on or when it would happen, and that meant he was nervous. It also meant that he was visiting his parents more often than usual, which was probably why his mother rolled her eyes when she saw him walk into her kitchen.

"What are you doing here?" she asked.

Lorcan huffed. "From your tone, it's almost as if you're not happy to see me."

"Of course I'm happy to see you. You're my son. But you were just here two days ago. And three days before that. What's going on?"

Lorcan had already tried bringing up the fact that he thought his parents should move out of Gillham for a bit. He understood it would be hard for them, but it would be safer. Of course, they were having none of that, especially his mom. "Is everything okay?" he asked instead of answering. She already knew what was going on. He didn't have to repeat it.

Her expression softened. "We're fine. We were fine two days ago, and we're still fine. I already told you I'm not worried about the guy planning on attacking the town. Kameron and the enforcers will keep Gillham safe."

"They're going to do everything they can, of course," Lorcan said as he leaned against the counter. "That doesn't mean they'll be able to, though. There are a lot of people in Gillham, Mom. Besides, the attack won't be something we can plan for. It's not like the man's going to call us and tell us that he's coming around."

She put down the towel she'd been drying her hands with and came to stand in front of Lorcan. "I know you're worried," she said.

Lorcan snorted. "Really? Because you've been ignoring what I was saying."

She shook her head. "I haven't been ignoring it. Your father and I talked. I told him what you told me, and we had a chat about what might happen and what we were ready to do to protect ourselves. If we need to, we'll hunker down in the house. Hell, we can even fly away and wait in a tree. But we're not leaving Gillham, Lorcan. We're not leaving you behind."

Lorcan swallowed. His parents were eagle shifters, just like he was, so if it came to that, they really could fly away and wait it out. Still. He was worried. What if Elroy attacked them by surprise? What if they didn't have time to shift and fly away? Lorcan didn't have an answer to that, and he didn't like it. He felt pulled in several directions, needing to protect his parents, his brother, and Devon. He didn't know where to focus, and he wanted to tell his parents that he'd found his mate. They wouldn't understand why he hadn't talked to him yet, though, so he'd kept his mouth shut, and he would continue to do so until he felt Devon was ready.

He wasn't sure that would ever happen.

His mom patted his shoulder. "Well, since you're here, you can take the trash out."

Lorcan groaned. "Why do I have to take the trash out? I don't even live here."

"You don't, but you're here enough that you might as well."

"That's not true. I haven't been sleeping here. I'm just visiting."

His mom arched a brow. "And eating my food. And using my couch and my TV. You contributed to the trash, so you can take it out."

Lorcan couldn't help but smile. He was still worried for his parents and his brother, and most of all, for Devon, but he knew there was nothing he could do. He was an enforcer, but he couldn't protect all of them. He had to work with his team, and he would. He just wished fear didn't cling to him like a bad stomachache.

Instead of continuing to protest, he moved toward the trashcan. It wasn't full yet, not as full as he'd allowed when he still lived with his parents. He was tempted to tell his mother that, but he knew it wouldn't go down well. She liked her house neat, and Lorcan wanted to help her, even if it was only by taking out the trash.

He took the bag out and turned, but his mom was already busy with the food again. He watched her for a moment, her hands flying over the cutting board, chopping the vegetables in small pieces. He had no idea what she was cooking, but he knew it would be good.

He missed this. He was an adult, but he missed living with his parents. He was grateful he had some privacy in the enforcers' building, but he also missed having a home. He wanted to do like Justin had and buy a house, settle down, but he wouldn't be able to do any of that until he knew what Devon wanted. He didn't want to buy a place for them to live if Devon didn't like it.

Lorcan shook his head. His life was complicated, and he couldn't see it becoming simpler anytime soon.

"Everything okay?" his mom asked, and Lorcan realized she'd stopped cutting the vegetables and was looking at him, worry in her gaze.

He forced himself to smile. "I'm perfectly fine. I was only trying to understand what you were cooking."

She looked from him to the vegetables. "Stew."

Lorcan grimaced. "I don't like stew."

"Then don't eat it."

He barked out a laugh. That had always been the way his mom dealt with meals. Even when they were kids, if they didn't like something, they didn't have to eat it, but they also wouldn't get anything else. He knew that if he wanted to have lunch or dinner with his family, he'd eat whatever his mom put on the table.

Even if it was stew.

He headed outside, leaving her to her vegetables. He dragged the trash bag toward the can, turning around when he heard a noise from the street. His heart raced, even though he realized it was stupid. The neighborhood was a perfectly fine neighborhood, and Elroy wasn't about to attack his parents.

Sure enough, it wasn't him. It was Liam, Lorcan's brother. He was getting out of his car. His gaze went straight to Lorcan, and he grinned. "I should have known you'd be here," he said.

Lorcan rolled his eyes. "What are *you* doing here?"

"Same thing as you. I'm hungry."

That wasn't why Lorcan was here, but he didn't want Liam to get worried. "It's stew."

"I don't like stew," Liam muttered.

Lorcan laughed. "That's what I said, and you know what

her answer was."

Liam grinned. "If we don't like it, we don't have to eat it, but we won't get anything else. I remember."

"What are you going to do? Stay here and watch them while they eat?"

Liam shook his head. "I might eat some bread. What about you? Are you leaving?"

Lorcan shrugged. "Maybe."

"After lunch, though, right?"

"Maybe," Lorcan repeated.

Liam peered at him. "What's going on?" he asked.

"Nothing."

"That's a lie, and you know it. Mom told me you've been around more often than usual. Is everything okay?"

Lorcan should tell him what was going on, but he didn't want to, not yet. He didn't want to talk to anyone about Devon, not when he wasn't sure Devon would want it. "I'm just worried about those people planning to attack the pack," he said instead, since he'd already told Liam about that.

Liam's expression shifted. "What does the pack have to say about it?"

"They don't know anything new. Nothing is going on, but I know they have people looking into it."

"You shouldn't worry about it too much, then. There's nothing you can do but be ready, and being hypervigilant all the time isn't going to help."

He was right. Lorcan knew it, but he couldn't help it.

"Anything else?" Liam asked, and Lorcan was glad for the distraction. Still, he wasn't about to tell Liam about Devon. His brother couldn't keep secrets to save his own life, and he would no doubt blurt it out in the middle of lunch, especially if he wasn't stuffing his mouth with food. Then Lorcan would have to answer a dozen questions from his parents, and he was *not* up to that today. "Nothing. Just worried."

Liam patted his shoulder. "I know. It's your job. Try to relax, though. It's not going to do you any good if you keep obsessing over this."

Once again, he was right, but Lorcan couldn't change anything. He wouldn't stop worrying because he couldn't. It was too easy for him to imagine what might happen to his family and Devon.

Devon couldn't stop thinking about Lorcan. He was starting to wonder if Yedley wasn't right about Lorcan being his mate, no matter how impossible it was.

Elroy had told him they were mates. That was one of the reasons Devon had agreed to date him. Then, once he'd been in a relationship with him, he hadn't been able to get out. On the one hand, he'd been terrified. Elroy didn't usually hit him, but he abused him in other ways. He also didn't hesitate to hurt him to punish him. The only time Devon had tried to break up with him, he'd had a black eye for several days afterward. He'd never tried again. The only other time he'd gone against Elroy was when he'd fled.

He was safe now, but he had so many questions and precisely zero answers.

He couldn't deny he'd never felt about Elroy the way he felt about Lorcan. He and Lorcan hadn't even had a conversation, yet Devon felt drawn to him. He wanted to talk to him, to find him and climb into his lap, to allow Lorcan to protect him and to love him. In Elroy's case, the only thing Devon had felt for him was anxiousness and fear, and now, hate. He wasn't sure he'd ever loved Elroy. He'd been stupid enough to believe him when he'd said they were mates, and he'd thought he owed it to him to give him a chance. He now knew he shouldn't have, but the past was the past, and he couldn't change it.

He *could* change the future, though.

It made sense to think Elroy had lied. Not only had Devon never felt drawn to him in any way, but it had always surprised him that Elroy didn't bond with him. Considering how controlling Elroy was, how jealous, it would have made sense. It would have given him something else to hold against Devon, and while Devon was relieved they'd never done it, he couldn't help but wonder why.

What if Elroy had lied? It wouldn't be the first time he lied to Devon. What if they truly weren't mates? What would it mean for Devon?

Devon had no idea. Staring out the window wouldn't help him find an answer, either, but he couldn't seem to be able to stop. It was the only way he got to see the world outside, and he took full advantage of it any time he could. Now, though, his thoughts were muddled, and every time he stopped forcing himself to think about something, in particular, they went back to Lorcan.

Could Devon trust him? He had no idea, and he didn't trust himself anymore. He had bad taste in men, even though he'd never loved Elroy. He'd still been with him, and he was ashamed just thinking about it. He wanted to believe that Lorcan was different, but could he?

Justin and Yedley seemed to think so. They liked Lorcan. They were friends with him. That much was enough to tell Devon that Lorcan wasn't a bad person. But what if Lorcan had lied to all of them? What if he was as bad as Elroy, and he was only better at keeping it hidden?

Devon shook his head. He shouldn't think that way. He didn't know Lorcan, and he should give him the benefit of the doubt.

He wasn't sure it would be enough, though.

He was aware that he needed to make a decision. Either he talked to Lorcan and asked him if they were mates, or he ignored the man and went his own way. That second option felt like the best one right now, but Devon knew it was fear speaking. If Lorcan was his mate and Elroy had lied to him, could Devon ignore the possibility of a future with Lorcan? And it wouldn't only take the bond away from Devon. It would take it away both from him and Lorcan, and that didn't feel fair.

Of course, it hadn't felt fair not to give Elroy a chance, either, and Devon had paid for that. But Lorcan hadn't even tried to talk to him. He hadn't tried to push him into anything. Hell, he hadn't told him they were mates, even though he knew Devon wouldn't find out on his own. He wasn't trying to influence Devon in any way. He wasn't like Elroy, and Devon could see it with his own two eyes.

It was still hard to wrap his mind around all of this. He didn't think he would ever be able to trust anyone, not even himself. It felt like everything was ruined for him when it came to relationships. He was still young, and he realized that eventually, he would fall in love again. He would get over his fear of Elroy, although it might take years. He suspected the consequences of the abuse would linger for a long time, and it was damaging Devon's life. If Lorcan and Devon were mates, Devon should give them a chance. The only reason he wasn't was that he was afraid, and he was afraid because of Elroy and what he'd done.

He sighed and rubbed his face. Thinking about it wasn't changing anything. It didn't make it easier for him to make a decision. Instead, his thoughts went around and around, and he still didn't know what to do. He was afraid, and he knew that wouldn't change anytime soon.

What was he supposed to do, then?

He had no idea, and he wasn't sure anything would change until and unless he talked to Lorcan. Maybe doing that would help. If anything, it would give him the certainty they were mates. Then, he could do whatever he needed and could with that information.

That was it, then. Devon needed to talk to Lorcan.

The thought terrified him, and he was more than happy to take his time doing it.

Instead of heading out, Devon took his cell phone from the bed. He hadn't turned it on since he'd left Elroy, and he didn't want to do it now. He was terrified Elroy would be able to find him through it. Still, he needed to check in on Cedric. They'd been friends, since Cedric was the boyfriend of someone who worked for Elroy. They'd both been abused, and Devon had tried to convince Cedric to come with him when he'd left. Cedric had refused, probably too afraid of going against his boyfriend's orders. Devon understood. He wasn't sure how he'd found the courage to leave Elroy behind, and he doubted he would have it a second time.

He took a deep breath, then turned the phone on. He'd made sure to charge it, and he was quick, selecting Cedric's number and calling him. Elroy wasn't particularly technological, but Devon wouldn't put it past him to try to find him through the phone. He worked with a lot of people, including hackers. He had to do this, but he had to do it fast.

"Devon?" Cedric suddenly asked from the other side of the phone.

Devon relaxed. "Cedric," he said. He sounded breathless, and he was. He hadn't really expected Cedric to answer. Elroy knew he and Devon were friends, and Devon wouldn't be surprised if he'd asked Cedric where he was. Elroy wouldn't hesitate to threaten Cedric or to hurt him, and the thought made Devon's stomach hurt.

"Why are you calling me?" Cedric asked. His voice was urgent, and from the sounds that he could hear, Devon could tell that he was moving.

"I needed to check on you," Devon explained.

"I'm fine. You're going to get both yourself and me killed if you continue contacting me, though."

Devon's chest squeezed. "What happened?"

"Nothing you didn't suspect would happen." Cedric hesitated. "Are you okay?"

"I'm fine. More than fine." Devon couldn't tell him where he was. He couldn't risk it. There might be something else he could do, though. "I'm safe. I have friends. We can help you get out."

There was a moment of silence, and Devon waited, holding his breath. He wanted Cedric to say yes, but he wasn't surprised when his friend didn't. "You know I can't do it," Cedric said.

"Why not? I managed to escape. So can you."

"I can't," Cedric insisted.

Devon knew Cedric's boyfriend had something against him, but he'd never been able to find out what it was. Cedric had never said anything, and Devon knew it wouldn't change, not now. He wanted to push, but he could hear the resolution in his friend's voice.

He sighed. "If you need anything, text me. Let me know. I'm turning my phone off again once we hung up, but I'll text you my new number." It was a risk. But Devon couldn't abandon Cedric.

"You can't. It's too dangerous."

"I don't care. I need to make sure you're okay." Because Devon wouldn't be here now if Cedric hadn't helped him escape. He wouldn't be free. He wanted to do the same for Cedric, and he would, no matter what it took.

Lorcan liked spending time with his family, but he was also glad to be able to go back to the enforcers' building once he was done. It had been hard to listen to his parents and his brother talk as if nothing was happening outside their little world. He understood why they needed to focus on their normal life, but it was hard for him, knowing that something terrible was about to happen.

He stopped his car in front of the building, wrinkling his nose at the way some of the other enforcers parked. When he left the car, he stretched and took a deep breath. He'd eaten the stew his mother had made after all, even though he wasn't crazy about it, and it sat in his stomach. It wasn't a bad sensation, and it sent him back to childhood, to a place of comfort and love. His family would be okay. They had to be. He would do everything he could to make sure they were, but unfortunately, he was only one man.

Something moved in the bushes, catching Lorcan's attention. He frowned and took a step closer, then stopped. It couldn't be an animal. Most wild animals stayed far away from pack territory. The wolves and other shifters who lived there wouldn't hurt them, but they didn't know that. They only knew that a high number of predators lived here, and they didn't want anything to do with them. The only wild animals who'd stuck around were birds and squirrels, but from the sound of it, it was something bigger.

What was going on?

Lorcan didn't think anyone had managed to sneak in, at least, not anyone who didn't belong, not with the pack security being higher than usual. They would have seen whoever had come in, even if it had been a Nix. Pack territory was shielded from Nix who didn't belong, just in case. It was a pain in the ass for some of them, and a few areas, like the infirmary, and of course, the enforcers' building, had to stay accessible to everyone. Maybe whoever was there had managed to sneak in through the gate or one of the spaces that weren't shielded.

A head popped between the bushes, and Lorcan took a step

back, sucking in a breath.

What was Devon doing here?

Lorcan had no idea, and he couldn't seem to be able to ask. He watched as Devon stepped out from the bushes. He smiled when he saw a few leaves were stuck in his hair, but he didn't say anything about it. He didn't think he would be able to speak.

Lorcan wouldn't find out why Devon was here until Devon told him, but his heart was racing. There was only one reason Devon could be here, wasn't there? He'd somehow found out that he and Lorcan were mates, and he wanted to know more about it.

Lorcan watched his mate has he carefully came closer. Devon kept looking around as if he expected someone to jump out from the bushes like he had and hurt him, and Lorcan wanted to tell him that he wouldn't allow anyone to do that. He didn't want to freak Devon out, though.

Devon finally stopped in front of Lorcan. He looked at his feet, then rubbed the back of his neck. He looked up again but seemed to be carefully avoiding looking Lorcan in the eyes.

That was okay with Lorcan. He understood it was probably easier and more comfortable for Devon to do this like that—whatever this was.

"Hello," Devon finally said.

Lorcan had to clear his throat. "Hello," he answered.

Devon smiled nervously. "Okay, so I want to start by saying that even though I snuck up on you, I'm not here to hurt you."

Lorcan couldn't help it—he laughed. "I know. You don't hurt people. You're not the type."

Devon frowned. "I'm sure I could if I wanted to."

From what Lorcan knew, Devon was the kind of person who wouldn't hurt a fly if he could help it, but he didn't want his mate to be offended. "Almost everyone can hurt someone if they need to. I suspect you're that kind of person. You'd hurt someone if you didn't have a choice, but you would never do it willingly."

Devon blinked. "I hadn't realized you knew me that well."

Lorcan hadn't, either. It was weird, especially considering how little time they'd spent together. "Justin talks about you a lot," he finally said.

Devon wrinkled his nose. "I can't imagine why. Doesn't he have better things to talk about?"

That made Lorcan laugh again. "It's a change from him talking about Yedley all the time. We're all grateful for it."

Devon grinned. "They talk about each other a lot, don't they?"

"Well, they love each other, so it makes sense."

The smile on Devon's lips dimed. "Right. They're in love, and they're mates. That's why they always talk about each other. That's why they're together."

"They're together because they're in love. Being mates doesn't mean you have to be with someone."

"But it does mean you should give him a chance. It wouldn't be fair otherwise, would it?"

Lorcan was convinced more than ever that Devon knew. He had to be careful with what he said. He didn't want Devon to feel obligated to be with him or even to talk to him, but he also didn't want to miss this chance. "I don't think mates owe anything to each other," he said slowly. "Of course, I'd want my mate to talk to me. I'd want to get to know him. I think that's the only way to know if you're compatible or not. But I can understand that some people have previous experiences that would mean they couldn't even try. I wouldn't want my mate to be unhappy and to force himself just because he thinks he has to do it."

"So you wouldn't mind if your mate didn't even want to talk to you?"

"I can't say I wouldn't mind. I would be hurt, of course. Mates are one in a million. I wouldn't ever get the chance to meet someone like him. But if it was what he needed, then I wouldn't push. Being with your mate isn't an obligation. It would hurt, but I would get over it eventually."

Devon blinked. "It's hard to talk about this when we're talking about hypotheticals."

"Maybe. I don't want to make you uncomfortable, though."

Devon shrugged and looked down again. "So you would want your mate to talk to you, but you wouldn't want him to feel obligated to do it. Did I get that right?"

Lorcan nodded. "You did. Like I said, it would hurt, but I would understand." Lorcan hesitated. "I have friends in the pack and with the enforcers. Some of them have been through a lot, and I know their stories. I realize how hard it can be to trust people, even to trust your mate. I understand why someone would want time and space, and I'd be ready to give my mate anything he needs."

"Even if it takes years?"

"Even then. You'll find that most people, especially people here with the pack, feel the same way. They've all been through a lot, although they haven't been through the same things. We understand it can be hard, and no one would push for anything."

"You're part of these people. You *truly* don't expect anything?"

"I don't." Lorcan wanted, though. He wanted Devon to come closer. He wanted his mate in his life. He wanted to make Devon happy.

He wasn't sure he could, though. He was aware of the trauma Devon had gone through. He'd heard Devon explain everything to Kameron, and he wasn't sure Devon would ever be able to come back from that. He wanted his mate to heal. He wanted his mate to be okay and happy, even if it meant Devon wasn't with him. It would hurt, but Lorcan would deal with it.

He would have to.

"I talked with Yedley the day you and the others came over for dinner," Devon said.

Lorcan swallowed. "And?"

"I told him what I felt for you. I told him I felt drawn to you, in a way I've never felt drawn to Elroy."

Lorcan held his breath. He wanted to ask questions, but he could see the wrong one would make Devon bolt.

Devon chuckled darkly and rubbed his face. "Yedley said I should talk to you and ask you if I was your mate. He said that since I'm human, it's the only way for me to be sure."

"He's right. You can't feel it the way a shifter can," Lorcan agreed.

This time, Devon looked straight at him. "Is it true, then? Am I your mate?"

Lorcan couldn't lie. "You are. We're mates, Devon."

Devon had expected it. He'd suspected Yedley was right and that he and Lorcan were mates because of how he felt for Lorcan, and now, he knew. Lorcan had confirmed it.

So of course, Devon panicked and turned around. He ran away, his heart racing in his chest. Lorcan called out for him, but he was relieved when Lorcan didn't come after him. He had no idea where he was going, but he knew he was safe. He was in pack territory. No one would hurt him, even if he wandered in the woods for the rest of the day.

He ran until he couldn't anymore. He ran until he was breathless—until his thoughts had finally cleared. Then he stopped.

He was panting, and he had to lean against a tree. He

looked around, both to make sure he was alone and to see where he was. He still had no idea, and the only thing he could see was trees.

He didn't know why he'd run. He'd wanted to talk to Lorcan some more, to ask him questions about the bond they shared, but he'd been overwhelmed. He needed space, and instead of being a normal person and talking to Lorcan, explaining that he needed some time, he'd run away like a child.

He huffed and shook his head. He was afraid — there was no denying that. He would always be afraid, especially when it came to men. But Lorcan was different. He was Devon's mate, and his words had settled something in Devon's mind. Lorcan wouldn't force him into anything. He'd been clear — if Devon didn't want anything to do with him, then that was okay. If it took Devon years to get used to having him in his life, to get used to the fact that they were mates and accepting it, that was fine, too.

Lorcan had been reasonable. Hell, he'd been perfect. And what had Devon done? He'd run away. He'd run as if Lorcan was telling him they had to bond right now and move in together.

He'd panicked. There was no other word for it, and if there was, Devon didn't want to find it. Panic was enough. It perfectly described the tightening of his chest, the way he couldn't breathe, the way his head swam with thoughts and feelings.

He looked around again. He was safe now — he'd always been safe, but his mind only seemed to realize it now — but he was alone, and he had no idea *where* he was. He needed to get home.

He took his cell phone out. It wasn't the old one, the one he'd used to call Cedric. Instead, it was a phone Justin and Yedley had bought for him. He'd tried telling them he didn't need one since he never left the house, but they'd insisted, and he was relieved they had. He didn't know how he would go home if he hadn't had it.

He dialed Yedley's number with trembling fingers and waited.

"How did it go?" Yedley asked when he answered.

Devon laughed. "As bad as it could have gone. I ran away." He didn't feel happy at all, but he couldn't seem to be able to stop giggling.

"Oh. What happened?"

"Nothing. I asked him what he would do if he found out his mate didn't want to talk to him, and he said it would be okay. He said he would understand, and that he wouldn't expect anything from his mate."

"Did you ask him if *you* are his mate?"

"I did, and he confirmed. We're mates." That, too, was hard to wrap his mind around. Devon had thought Elroy was his mate for so long that it was weird to have someone else step into that role.

Of course, Lorcan hadn't *actually* said he wanted to. He'd told Devon he would give him time, but after what had just happened, Devon wouldn't be surprised if Lorcan decided he was too much work. He knew he was. He was a mess, and that wasn't going to change anytime soon.

"You panicked," Yedley said.

"I did. I know I should have stayed there and talked to him, but instead, I turned around and ran away."

"He won't care."

Devon wasn't sure that was the case, but he couldn't face it right now. "I'm in the forest, and I have no idea where. Can you come to get me?"

"Only if you're in a spot where I can shimmer. Try to get back to the enforcers' building, or to the infirmary. There are paths around, so you should be able to find your way."

Devon hadn't even realized there were paths, but after

looking around for a few minutes, he finally found one. There was even a sign and an arrow that told him the infirmary wasn't far. He sighed in relief. "Okay. I found a sign for the infirmary," he told Yedley.

"Good. I'll hang up, and I'll be there in seconds. Don't freak out."

It was a bit late for that, but Devon agreed anyway. "I'll be fine," he said, and he realized he was trying to convince himself as much as he was trying to convince Yedley.

He found his way to the infirmary. It didn't look like an infirmary, but rather, like a nice little house in the woods. He didn't have time to examine it further, though, because Yedley was already waiting for him. Devon had never been so grateful to see his friend. He took the hand Yedley offered and squeezed it, holding onto it like a lifeline.

"You're okay?"

Devon nodded, even though he felt anything but okay. "I'll be fine. Take me home, please."

Yedley did. They shimmered in the entrance, and Devon could hear Justin was talking to someone. When he listened more carefully, he realized it was a phone call, because he could only hear Justin's voice. Yedley didn't let go of Devon's hand. Instead, he dragged him to the living room, where Justin was pacing, his phone by his ear. He looked up when he heard Devon and Yedley, and Devon saw him relax. "Okay. He's here," he said to whoever he was talking to.

Yedley leaned closer to Devon. "Lorcan called him just as I was shimmering out. He was worried about you," he murmured.

And now, Devon felt even more guilty. "He was worried?"

"Of course he was. You're his mate. He might not expect anything from you, but he does want to make sure you're okay and safe."

Devon turned his attention back to Justin, who was still on

the phone.

"He seems to be fine, but I'm going to make sure. Don't freak out, Lorcan. He's okay. I don't know what happened, but I'm sure you didn't do anything." He paused and listened to whatever Lorcan was saying. Devon wished he were a shifter so he could hear the other side of the conversation. But he was just a human, and he had to make do with what he had. "I'll text you if anything comes up," Justin said.

Devon felt like an asshole. He shouldn't have run. He shouldn't have freaked out.

"What happened?" Justin asked softly.

Devon realized he'd hung up. He shook his head. He didn't want to talk about it. He already had. Still, Justin and Yedley were his only friends, and if he couldn't talk to them, who could he talk to? "When Elroy and I met, he told me we were mates. That's why I decided to give him a chance. I thought that since we were destined to be together, it wouldn't be so bad, that *he* wouldn't be so bad." Devon never wanted to repeat this story again, and he hoped it would be the last time.

Justin's expression changed, and he gently steered Devon toward the couch. "It was a lie," he said.

Devon nodded. "Lorcan confirmed I'm *his* mate. That means Elroy was lying the entire time and that I stayed with him for nothing."

"You stayed with him because he was abusing you. You didn't have a choice."

"I should have known he was lying to me. I shouldn't have let him guilt me into being with him in the first place. I was an idiot."

"You weren't an idiot. You thought you were doing the right thing, and you couldn't know he was lying back then. Give yourself some slack, Devon. Nobody is perfect, not even you."

Devon buried his face in his hands. "What am I supposed

to do now? I ran away like an idiot. Even if Lorcan wanted anything to do with me before, I doubt it's still the case."

"You're wrong. He was worried about you. He wanted to make sure you'd made it home safe. No matter what you think, Lorcan cares about you."

He was right. Devon knew that. Even if it was only because of the bond, Lorcan did care about him.

If only Devon knew what to do about all of this.

CHAPTER THREE

Lorcan was disappointed, but most of all, he was worried about Devon. He hadn't believed his eyes when he'd seen Devon waiting for him when he'd come back home, and he'd been tempted to run after his mate once Devon had fled. He almost had, too, and he probably would have if Tanner hadn't come out of the house right then. He'd told Lorcan to give Devon time, and Lorcan had to agree it had been the best thing to do.

Nothing would hurt Devon in pack territory. No matter how long he ran, he would always find his way back. Pack territory was fenced, and even though people could freely come in and out through the entrance, the forest was safe.

Still, Lorcan had been relieved when Justin had called him. Devon was home, and Lorcan had been able to relax.

Except he hadn't. He still wasn't relaxed, even though a few days had passed. He couldn't help but wonder why Devon had run away the way he had. Was it because of something Lorcan had said or done? Lorcan couldn't remember anything except that he'd told Devon they were mates. He'd admitted it when Devon had asked about it, and he didn't regret it. Devon had deserved to know, especially since he already suspected.

Why had he left, though? Maybe he didn't want Lorcan as a mate. Lorcan wouldn't be surprised. After everything Devon had gone through, he probably didn't want a mate, period. Even if he *did* want someone in his life, maybe he didn't like Lorcan. Lorcan had always done his best to be a good

40

person and to give Devon space, but that didn't mean Devon liked him that way. Maybe he just wanted to be Lorcan's friend. Maybe he didn't like the way Lorcan looked, and Lorcan wasn't his type.

Except he should be. They were mates. That meant they were perfect for each other, and that included physically. Lorcan found Devon gorgeous and sexy. Devon should feel the same about him, and Lorcan wasn't quite sure what to do with the knowledge that he might not.

"You're still moping?" Tanner asked from the living room entrance.

Lorcan blinked and looked up at him. "I'm not moping."

Tanner rolled his eyes. "You are. But that's fine. I might not know what happened, but it's your right to mope, especially since you're not on duty."

Lorcan scowled at him, even though he wasn't angry. He was irritated, though. "Did you want something?"

"Actually, I did. There's someone at the door for you."

Lorcan had no idea who would want to see him. His parents and his brother had his phone number, so they could call him if they needed anything. No one ever visited him at the enforcers building. When they met, it was usually at Justin's house, mostly because it was more comfortable and there weren't other enforcers around. "I don't want to talk to whoever it is," Lorcan said. Whatever it was, it could wait.

He needed to mope some more.

Tanner shook his head. "Trust me. You're going to want to talk to him."

Lorcan truly didn't want to get up from the couch. He wanted to tell Tanner to fuck off, and to take whoever was disturbing him with him. He knew better than to do that, though. Tanner would never let him live it down, especially if it was important.

Besides, Lorcan couldn't deny he was curious. He *was*

moping, so maybe it was time for him to distract himself. This might be what he needed, as long as he could stop thinking about Devon for a bit.

He begrudgingly rose from the couch. "Fine. I'm going."

Tanner's smile widened. "Good. I'm here if you need me, although I doubt that will be the case."

"I'm not sure what you're trying to say, but I don't like it," Lorcan said as he passed by him.

Tanner's chuckle followed him to the front door. It was open, and Lorcan stepped out, blinking at the sunlight. His eyes widened when he saw Devon was waiting for him on the porch, looking away from the house. He was staring at the forest, and he was tapping his fingertips on the porch rail as if he was nervous.

If he was anything like Lorcan, he no doubt was.

Lorcan cleared his throat, and Devon jumped, twisting around to look at him. Lorcan had no idea what to do, so he stupidly raised a hand and waved. "I didn't expect you," he said.

That was stupid, too. Of course he hadn't expected Devon.

Devon rubbed the back of his neck and looked away. "I didn't expect to come, either. I wasn't sure I would be able to until now. You don't know how many times I thought about running away again."

Lorcan frowned. "We don't have to talk if you don't want to. I'll understand."

Devon shook his head. "I'm sure you would, but I do want to talk. I won't run away again."

"I see," Lorcan said even though he didn't. He didn't know why Devon was here. He didn't know what Devon wanted or how the conversation would end.

The only thing he *did* know was that he wanted to have it. He wanted Devon to be able to talk to him if he needed to, and he clearly did. Besides, he might be able to reassure

Devon some more about what he expected from him.

Lorcan wasn't sure why Devon had run the other day, whether it was because he didn't like him and didn't want him as a mate or because those words reminded him of Elroy, but whichever it was, he would do everything he could to make Devon feel better.

Someone moved behind him, and he turned around to see Tanner staring at him. Tanner grinned, then gestured for Lorcan to step out on the porch. He made kissy sounds, and Lorcan rolled his eyes.

"Why don't we go for a walk?" he suggested as he finally stepped closer to Devon.

Devon looked around. "A walk?"

Lorcan realized what might be going through Devon's head. "We won't go far, so you can come back anytime you want, and you can scream, and someone will come."

The corner of Devon's lips curled. "Why would I want to scream?"

Lorcan shrugged. "I don't know. I'm not going to do anything that might make you scream, but just in case, I want you to know you'll be safe." The only reason Lorcan didn't want to stick around was that there was always someone listening in the house. It might not always be one of his team members, but that didn't mean people weren't around. He wanted this conversation to be private, and he had no doubt the same went for Devon.

Devon looked from the house to the forest, and finally, at Lorcan. "We can go for a walk," he agreed.

Lorcan relaxed. He hadn't realized how nervous he was, but now he did, and he was relieved that Devon seemed to be trusting him, at least in part.

He gestured at the porch steps. "After you," he said.

Devon smiled, and it made him even more gorgeous. It made Lorcan wanted to move closer, to draw him into his arms.

Instead, he tightened his hands into fists so he wouldn't be tempted to touch Devon, and he allowed Devon to walk down the steps ahead of him. He followed, unable to look away.

He had no idea what was about to happen, but whatever it was, he would make sure Devon was happy at the end of it.

Devon wanted to run away, but then, that was what he always did, wasn't it? He'd run away from Elroy instead of trying to solve things. He doubted he would have been able to solve anything with Elroy. With a man like that, either you listened to him, or you paid.

But Devon could have done more. He could have gone to the police and told them what Elroy was doing. He could have gone to the council and told them about it—and he had, but he couldn't ignore the feeling that it might have been too late. He could have saved Cedric as well as himself. Instead, he'd left his only friend behind, and he'd run.

He wasn't going to run away this time. He couldn't, not when a chance at happiness was just within his reach.

If only he knew what to say. He'd been rehearsing the words he would tell Lorcan when he'd left the house with Yedley, but they seemed to have fled his mind. He'd talked both to Yedley and Justin, and they'd been nice. They always were. They'd pointed out that Lorcan was worried, and that Devon should call him to tell him he was okay, at the very least. They would never push him into doing anything, but even Devon had managed to see that just calling would have been wrong. After what Devon had done, after the way he'd run away yet one more time, Lorcan deserved an explanation—and a face to face one.

Devon cleared his throat and rubbed his hands on his

thighs. His palms were damp, and he was grateful Lorcan wasn't trying to hold his hand. It was way too soon for them to do that, especially given how Devon had reacted.

Lorcan was just walking, looking around and smiling at Devon when their gazes caught. He hadn't demanded to know why Devon was here, and he wasn't saying anything. He was giving Devon time, and Devon was glad. He felt like he didn't deserve it, but he had it, and he would take advantage of it.

He cleared his throat again, then steeled himself. "I wanted to apologize," he said.

Lorcan took a second to answer. "Why?"

Devon blinked at him. "What do you mean, why?"

"Exactly what I said. I want to know why you're apologizing to me."

"I thought it was obvious. For what I did the other day. I shouldn't have run away."

Lorcan shook his head. "I'm not angry at you for running away. I also don't think you shouldn't have done it. If that was what you felt like, then it's okay."

"But you were worried about me. Justin told me."

"I *was* worried. But I also realize that you probably need time, which is why I didn't go after you. I wanted to make sure you were okay. I suspected you would react badly when and if I told you that you were my mate, and I didn't expect you to find that out by yourself."

Devon was slightly angry. He understood why Lorcan hadn't wanted to tell him. His reaction was explanation enough. Still, they were in this together. They were each other's mates, and it wasn't right that only Lorcan would know.

But that wasn't the case anymore. Devon knew now, too, and what had he done with the knowledge? He'd left. "Anyway, I just wanted to apologize."

"Well, thank you. Even though I don't think you need to, I *am* grateful for the opportunity to see you. Justin told me you were okay, but I don't think I believed it until I saw you on the porch, not entirely."

"You needed to see it with your own two eyes."

Lorcan nodded. "I think so. A mate bond is always complicated, especially so for the shifter." He paused. "Especially so when their mate is a human. Humans do feel the bond, but not the same way, and it can get complicated."

Devon snorted. "I don't think it gets more complicated than me."

Lorcan smiled. "You would be surprised. I live with the enforcers, and over the years, I've seen many of them find their mates. It's never easy, but some of them believe there's a reason they meet their mate when they do, and I tend to believe the same."

Devon blinked. "So you think we met now for a reason? Not because of a coincidence?"

"I don't know. I don't think anyone can, not for sure. But yes. What were the odds that you ran away from your abusive ex-boyfriend and you ended up here, in Gillham, where I am, too?"

He wasn't wrong. It could be a coincidence, but there were several of them piling up, and Devon had never believed in them. He especially didn't believe in them now that he knew what Elroy had done, how he had fooled him. Now that he thought about it, he realized that several times, Elroy shouldn't have known where Devon was, not in the beginning. He shouldn't have been there to meet him and to seduce him. Instead, he had been, and now, Devon shuddered at the thought. He'd thought he'd had a choice back then, but he hadn't, not since the very beginning.

That brought him to something else he needed to tell Lorcan. "You know about Elroy, of course," he started.

"I was there when you explained to Kameron what happened, yes."

Devon sucked in a breath. He didn't like talking about Elroy, but he knew he needed to. "I know you're not him. You're nothing like him, and I realize that. It's one of the reasons I shouldn't have run away. I already knew you wouldn't react the way he did, but my instinct took over. I had to run. I was freaking out."

"You have nothing to apologize for," Lorcan repeated.

Devon was trying to say something, though. He *needed* to say it. "He told me I was his mate," he confessed. "I had no way to know whether or not that was true. I'm a human. I might feel the bond with you, but until now, I didn't realize I would. I heard the stories, of course, but still. I thought it was something that would come with time. Knowing I was his mate is the main reason I gave him a chance and stayed with him for so long. I realize now that he was lying, and I feel like an idiot."

"You shouldn't. He played you, and you had no way to know. You're not an idiot. You were hoping to have what so many people have, and I can't blame you. I do kind of want to strangle him, though."

To his own surprise, Devon laughed. "Well, you're going to have to get in line, because you're not the only one." He was terrified of Elroy, and he was pretty sure that if their paths ever crossed again, he would cower, but that didn't matter. Right now, he wanted to hurt Elroy for what he'd done, for how he'd ruined Devon's life for so long, and how he was still ruining it. It was Elroy's fault if Devon wasn't open with Lorcan. It was his fault that he was afraid to try and to trust his mate.

Devon swallowed. "So you see, even though I'm aware that you're not like Elroy, I don't know if I can trust my instincts right now. I allowed Elroy to push me around and hurt me. I allowed him to lie to me. I wanted to believe that things would change once we fell in love, but we never did. And once I was in, I couldn't get away." Elroy wouldn't have allowed it.

"And now, I come around and tell you we're mates," Lorcan said.

"Exactly. Even though I talked with Justin and Yedley and they told me that you're a good person, and I want to believe it, I don't know if I can. I don't know if I can give us a chance. I want to, but I don't even trust myself anymore, especially not when it comes to men."

"I understand," Lorcan said.

Devon detested that he did. He shouldn't have to. Devon should be strong, and he should realize that Lorcan had nothing to do with Elroy. He should know that Lorcan would never hurt him and that he could trust him.

And he did. But then, why was he so hesitant to do this?

When Lorcan had said that he wanted to strangle Elroy, he wasn't joking. If he ever got his hands on that man, he was going to make him pay for everything he'd done to Devon.

He wasn't surprised Elroy had lied to Devon. He should have realized that was what had happened. It made sense. Elroy would have wanted as much control over Devon as he could have and telling him they were mates allowed him that. Devon couldn't know if it was true, and that meant he would stay until he couldn't, until he was pushed to the point of breaking.

Which was what had happened. Devon had stayed with Elroy way too long, and now, Lorcan knew one of the reasons why. He despised Elroy for ruining this, both for him and Devon. He wanted Devon to trust him. Why wouldn't he? They were mates, and Devon was *supposed* to trust him. But all that trust had been ruined by one man, and Lorcan didn't know what to do.

He realized he would need to take things slow. That was the only way to show Devon he wasn't lying, and that he truly was a better man than Elroy. Hell, that wasn't hard. Elroy wasn't even decent. He was an asshole. He was planning to attack the pack and take over the town. Elroy would do everything he could to ruin Gillham and the pack, and he wouldn't stop until he got what he wanted, unless someone stopped him first.

Lorcan wouldn't have a problem being that person.

Right now, though, he needed to focus on Devon. It had taken him a lot of courage to come up to him and tell him what had happened. Lorcan had seen it from the beginning, in the way Devon trembled, in the way he looked like he wanted to run away. It was probably what he still wanted to do, but he hadn't, not this time. Instead, he'd stayed with Lorcan and he'd told him why he had run, what had happened to him in the past to make him react the way he had.

And now that Lorcan knew what had happened, maybe he could change the future. He could get Devon to see he was a trustworthy person, and hopefully, he could get Devon to fall in love with him. He wanted to fall in love with Devon, too. He wanted them to be happy together, as happy as Justin and Yedley. It wouldn't be easy, but he was ready to work for it.

"I'm not lying," he said quietly.

Devon startled. "I know that."

"Do you? Because I wouldn't blame you if that's what you're afraid of. I have no way to show you that we truly are mates, not until we bond." And then Devon would know, because they would be tied together for the rest of their lives. They would be able to feel each other's feelings, their emotions, and there would be no more doubts. In the meantime, though, there was no way for him to know that Lorcan was telling the truth.

Devon shook his head. "I *know* you're not lying. I never felt this way toward Elroy, even though I gave it my all." His cheeks flushed, but he continued. "When you told me we were mates, I had a hard time believing it. I'd always heard the stories of humans meeting their mates, of how they felt about that person. They felt drawn to them. They wanted to be with them always. I never felt that way with Elroy. Sure, he was attractive, but that was where things stopped. I would never have given him a second glance if he hadn't come up to me and told me we were mates. And even then, I tried to take things slow. I wasn't sure what to make of him, but I wanted to believe him." He paused.

Lorcan wanted to help him. He wanted to tell him it was okay, that he didn't have to talk if he didn't want to or if he didn't feel up to it. Instead, he waited. It didn't matter how long he would have to wait. Devon deserved to have all the time in the world to wrap his mind around what he was saying and what was happening.

"I grew up in foster care," Devon finally said. "I never had a family or parents. I guess that's one of the reasons I gave Elroy a chance and stuck with him much longer than I should have. I wanted to have that. I wanted to belong with someone, and since I was his mate, I belonged with him, right?" Devon shook his head. "But of course, that was a lie. I know it now, and it explains why I never felt anything for him. I shouldn't have stayed with him, but by the time I realized that it was too late."

Lorcan tightened his hands into fists. He wanted to hit something, but that was the best way to freak Devon out, and it was the last thing he wanted. He needed Devon to see him as different from Elroy. He wanted Devon to trust him, to trust that he would never hurt him, either physically or mentally. Of course, they would eventually fight if they ended up together, just like every other couple, but Lorcan would never be abusive.

"What now?" Lorcan asked after a while.

Devon shrugged. "Honestly? I have no idea. I wasn't sure what would happen when I came here, so I didn't make plans. I just wanted to get through this conversation and tell you everything I had to say. Now I feel strangely empty, and I think I need to reassess what's going to happen next."

"Nothing needs to happen next," Lorcan told him. "I don't expect anything from you."

Devon eyed him. "How can you not expect anything?"

"I don't expect anything from you. I hope something will happen, of course. I hope that eventually you'll be able to trust me fully. I hope you'll get to know me, and that you'll fall in love with me. I hope we'll bond, and that we'll have a happy life together. But I don't *expect* any of that. I understand what happened with your ex, and I can see why it would make you wary of giving me a chance. I won't berate you for that or hold it against you. You have to take your time and do things at your own pace. *That's* what will make me happier."

Devon bit his lower lip. "How can you say that me taking my time will make you happy? I'm your mate. Don't you want to be with me?"

"More than anything. But I also don't want to hurt you. I want you to feel like you have a choice, because you do. I'm not going to force you to stay with me just because you're my mate. I want you to *want* to be with me. I want you to love me and for that to be the reason you stick around." Lorcan swallowed. He was saying too much. He didn't want to scare Devon, but he felt like Devon needed to know. "We can start slow if you want. You can go home and stay away for a while, think about what we just said to each other. We can have a coffee, have another conversation and see where things go."

To Lorcan's surprise, Devon smiled. "I can do coffee."

"Great." It was more than Lorcan had expected.

"How are we getting there? Because I didn't drive here. Yedley shimmered me."

Lorcan blinked. He hadn't meant that they should have coffee now, but eventually, after Devon had the time to wrap his mind around what was happening. He wasn't about to tell Devon that, though. "We can go back to the enforcer's building. My car is parked there. Or we can walk. It's not that far." And it would give them more time to talk. Lorcan never wanted to stop, and he wasn't looking forward to the moment in which Devon would have to go home tonight.

Devon's smile was gorgeous. "We can walk. I've been cooped up in Justin's house for a while, and I need to stretch my legs." His cheeks reddened even more. "Of course, the reason I've been stuck there is my own fault, but still."

He felt safe with Lorcan. The realization gave Lorcan's heart a little jolt, and he couldn't help but smile. "Walking it is, then. It won't take long." Lorcan wasn't sure what they were going to talk about, because he was terrified to hurt Devon or to say the wrong thing, but they could figure this out together.

Together. Lorcan hadn't thought they would share anything, but it looked like they might have a chance after all.

Devon felt awkward. The last time he'd had a first date, it had been with Elroy, and it hadn't gone well. That should have been the first sign Devon should run away instead of sticking around.

He despised Elroy. He despised him for lying, for forcing him to stick around even when he hadn't wanted to. He despised him even more for almost taking this away from him. If Devon didn't manage to get over his fear, he would never know how having a mate really was. The only thing he would have was his experience with Elroy, and that didn't count since they hadn't truly been mates.

But he *was* Lorcan's mate. He was sure of that. He could feel it in his bones, and he didn't want to do anything wrong. He wanted this to work, even though he didn't know how to make that happen. He wanted him and Lorcan to have a chance, but the problem was that he wasn't sure they did. They were starting at a disadvantage. Devon had trusted the wrong man, and even though Lorcan had nothing to do with it, Devon wasn't sure he would ever be able to trust his mate. He was going to try, of course. He would work as hard as he could and should to make sure that happened, but he couldn't help but wonder if Elroy had ruined him for everyone else, including Lorcan. Sometimes, he felt that way. He felt like he would never go back to a normal life. He was always afraid, always expecting Elroy to jump out of the shadows to drag him home. He never wanted to go back. He wanted to forget about Elroy and to never see him again.

Maybe meeting Lorcan was Devon's chance at a second life and a new start. Maybe that was why he'd met Elroy in the first place. He wouldn't have ended up in Gillham if he hadn't, and he would never have met Lorcan. Or maybe he would have in another way. But Devon should focus on the present, on having that coffee with Lorcan and on finding something to talk about.

It was hard, though. He didn't trust himself not to make bad decisions, especially when it came to boyfriends. Elroy was the worst decision he'd ever made, and he was terrified to make another one, maybe a worse one. He didn't know how to act with Lorcan. Even before Elroy, he hadn't had that much experience. He'd only had a few boyfriends, and none of them had been serious. Elroy, on the other hand, had been as serious as a heart attack, and not in a good way. Those experiences left Devon floundering, and he wasn't sure how to get out of it. What did one talk about when they were walking with their mates? It wasn't even a first date, and Devon had no idea what to do.

"You said you grew up in foster care," Lorcan began.

Devon could have kissed him. "I did."

"Do you want to talk about that? Can you talk about it without feeling sad?"

Devon shrugged. "I guess. I was one of the lucky ones. I wasn't abused, not beyond a few slaps and some yelling."

Lorcan grimaced. "I wouldn't call that lucky."

"Maybe not, but I knew a lot of kids who had it much worse than me. Really, I was lucky. I was never abused, not until Elroy, and I even managed to get in contact with my sister."

Lorcan smiled. "You have a sister?"

"I do." Devon hesitated. "But I haven't seen her since I met Elroy. He made sure that I didn't talk to her. He pushed her and everyone else away and isolated me."

"Because that way, you would be even more under his control."

"Exactly. And since I left, I've been afraid to contact her. I think he knows that I might go to her, or at the very least, that I would talk to her. Her not knowing what happened and where I am is probably safest for both of us." Even though it hurt him.

"It's not fair, though."

Devon snorted. "But life isn't fair, is it? Anyway, like I told you, I was one of the lucky ones. I wasn't adopted, but none of the foster families I spent time with really hurt me. They neglected me for the most part, but that was okay."

Lorcan looked like he wanted to disagree, and Devon didn't blame him. But people who hadn't gone through foster care couldn't understand. He'd seen horrible things. He'd talked to people who had been hurt, *really* hurt. What he'd gone through was nothing next to that, and he knew how lucky he'd been to escape foster care at eighteen with no deep trauma. But then he'd fucked it up and had chosen to be with Elroy. He truly was an idiot sometimes.

"You should contact your sister," Lorcan said.

Devon wanted nothing more. "I think I will, eventually."

"You know where she is, then?"

"I do. She was adopted."

Lorcan's expression horrified. "I thought that people adopted siblings together."

Devon shook his head. "They do try to keep siblings together. But she's significantly younger than me, and she was a baby when we were taken away from my mom. She found adoptive parents right away. I wasn't that lucky. Still, her parents are wonderful, and we kept in touch." She was what had helped Devon so much during the long hours in which Elroy was abusing him, when desperation had threatened to take over. She'd given Devon something to work toward, a light in the darkness, and he would never be able to thank her enough. She didn't even know she'd done it because he hadn't talked to her in so long. He was planning to change that, but he had to make sure he was safe and that Elroy wouldn't use her and hurt her to get to him.

"What about you? Do you have siblings?" he asked so they would talk about something else. He could see Lorcan was working himself up over what had happened to him, and he didn't want that. It was over. He was an adult now, even though he continued to make mistakes. Lorcan didn't have to worry about it or to pity him.

Lorcan smiled. "I have a brother. He and my parents both live in town."

"You see them often?"

"More often now that I know the town is in danger. I've tried convincing them to leave, at least for a while, but they won't hear it. They're convinced the enforcers and Kameron will be able to protect both the pack and the town."

"And you don't think so?"

Lorcan hesitated. "I want to believe we'll be able to. I'll do everything I can to make sure that everyone here is safe. But there are only so many of us. We don't know when Elroy will strike. This is a waiting game, and I hate it. We know Elroy is going to strike soon, but how soon? There's no way to know."

The information Devon had managed to get to them wasn't enough. Devon bit his lower lip, wondering if there was anything he'd missed, anything that could help, but he couldn't think of anything. He'd told Kameron everything there was to know, and he couldn't do anything else.

Not for Gillham, anyway.

"But enough talking about that," Lorcan said. "I want to talk about something good. I don't want us to start being all doom and gloom. We both know that there's danger waiting, but it doesn't mean we have to stop living. Come on. Tell me what your plans are after this is over."

Devon had no idea, but Lorcan wasn't wrong. He didn't want to think about what Elroy was going to do, not for a bit. He didn't know if this was their first date or just a coffee between friends, but he wanted to take advantage of it. He wanted to get to know Lorcan, to be able to relax finally. The fear would still be here when he went home tonight, and tomorrow, when he woke up. But for this afternoon, he wanted to focus on Lorcan and the future he hoped they would have together.

CHAPTER FOUR

Lorcan was hopeful. For the first time in what felt like forever, he knew things would be okay. He knew everyone would be safe.

Or at least, that was what he felt like. It had a lot to do with how he felt about Devon. After the coffee they'd had together, they'd exchanged numbers, and they'd been texting and calling each other since then. It hadn't been that long, only a few weeks, but when Devon had told Lorcan he wanted to see him again, Lorcan had jumped on the opportunity, and now, they had their first date planned.

Lorcan wasn't sure whether or not it really was their first date. The coffee date had felt like a date, and they'd talked a lot about their lives and what they expected from the future. Devon's answers had been painful. He wanted to feel safe and to be able to live his life the way he wanted, and Lorcan desperately wished he could give him that. He hoped that in time he would, and that their date on Saturday was the first step toward that. He would do everything he could so Devon felt safe with him.

It was almost a week to wait, though, and he was starting to get nervous. It wasn't his *first* first date, but it would be his last one, and he wasn't sure how to feel about that. Happy, that was for sure. He never wanted to have another first date, not after Devon. But he knew things might not work out. Devon might be too afraid, to unsure. He might never trust Lorcan, and Lorcan would have to face that.

Not now, though. For now, things seemed to be working

out, albeit slowly, and Lorcan wasn't going to question it. If things went wrong, he would face them when the time came. In the meantime, though, he needed to focus on the future and on having Devon in it.

He walked into his parents' kitchen, whistling. He was meeting his mom to take her grocery shopping—something she had agreed on only because she wanted to see him. She usually did the shopping on her own, but Lorcan didn't want her to be alone around town. Several weeks had passed since Devon had arrived in Gillham, and Elroy still hadn't done anything. A few of the people who had been undercover with the Beasts, the gang Elroy was working with, had come back, and they'd had information, but it hadn't helped. They knew what Elroy was planning, but they didn't know when.

Lorcan doubted it would take much longer, though. He wished this was over already. He wasn't looking forward to having to fight and possibly kill people, to having his family and the people he cared for in danger, but this waiting and hoping was destroying him. He needed this to be over so he could focus on the future, and so did the rest of the town.

"You're awfully chipper this morning," his mom said.

She was sitting at the breakfast nook, sipping on coffee and reading her tablet—no doubt a newspaper, if Lorcan knew her.

He grinned at her. Even though he didn't like waiting and wondering what Elroy was doing, he couldn't deny he was happy. It was easy to forget about the danger when he focused on Devon. "Shouldn't I be?" he asked.

Her eyes narrowed, and she put down her tablet. "You should be. I always want you to be happy. Something happened, though, right?"

Lorcan wanted to tell her. He'd never wanted anything more, except when it came to Devon. He wasn't sure what Devon would think about it, though. They hadn't talked about it, and even though Justin and Yedley knew and Devon didn't seem to have a problem with that, Lorcan didn't want to do something wrong.

He was grateful for the distraction when his father stepped into the kitchen, at least until he saw the suitcase through the open door to the entrance. He frowned. "Dad?"

His father smiled at him. "Just a business trip. Don't worry."

On the one hand, that would mean Lorcan's father was safe and away from Gillham. On the other, it would mean that Lorcan's mother would be alone in the house. "How long?" he asked.

"I'll be back in a few days. I already told Liam, and he's going to come around. I expect you to do the same thing, and we already told the neighbors. They didn't quite understand why we were acting this way when it's not my first business trip, but they agreed to keep an eye on your mother."

Lorcan's mom huffed. "As if I need keepers."

Lorcan was relieved, even though he wished his mother would go with his father. "We'll keep her safe," he said.

His father nodded. "I know. Anything new with you?"

"He came in whistling," Lorcan's mother said.

Lorcan playfully glared at her. "Are you going to reveal all my secrets?"

"I don't know any of your secrets. You haven't even told me why you're so happy."

Lorcan sucked in a breath. He wanted to tell them, and what would it change? They ought to know whether or not things went well with Devon. If things went badly, they would notice Lorcan was sad. They would want to know what happened, and they would find out. And if things worked out with Devon, then Lorcan wanted them to be happy for him. He wanted them to get to know Devon when the time came.

"Something did happen," he eventually said.

His mom put her coffee down, too, which was a clear sign that she was listening to him.

Lorcan had to swallow a few times. His mouth was dry, and he wasn't sure why. He was nervous, even though he knew his parents would be happy for him. He cleared his throat, then finally managed to get the words out. "I met my mate."

There was a moment of silence in which his parents stared at him. Then, his mother burst out of her chair and rushed toward him, her arms open. Lorcan laughed when she wrapped herself around him, and he hugged her back. "I'm so happy for you," she said.

"We both are," Lorcan's father added.

Lorcan's mom leaned back, but she didn't let him go. "Who is he? When can we meet him? Where did you meet?"

Lorcan laughed again and shook his head. "I won't be able to tell you anything if you don't let me speak."

She mimed locking her mouth and throwing away the key, and Lorcan couldn't help but smile. His heart felt lighter than it had in a long time, and he hoped things would continue that way. Still, he needed to explain that the situation was complicated.

He rubbed the back of his neck. "His name is Devon. He's currently living with Justin and Yedley, and that's not going to change anytime soon. It's also going to be a while before you can meet him." His mom opened her mouth, no doubt to argue, but Lorcan shook his head. "It's not because I don't want you to meet him. He was abused, and he ran away from his abuser. That man told him they were mates. I think he believes me when I tell him he's my mate, but I don't want to push him. I never want to do anything to hurt him, not after what he went through. That means we're going to take our time. We've been talking and texting, and we have our first date this weekend. As soon as he feels up to meeting you, I'll introduce you. But in the meantime, you're going to have to wait."

"That won't be a problem," Lorcan's father said. "We're both happy you found your mate, and we look forward to meeting him, but we understand how complicated things can be. Take care of him and make sure he's comfortable and happy. We can wait all the time he needs to get to know him. He's not going anywhere, and neither are we."

Lorcan hoped his father was right. He wanted Devon to see they could have a future together, to give him a chance, but he knew that might never happen. Even if they dated, Devon might still get scared or realize this wasn't what he wanted. Lorcan wouldn't blame him for it. He would be hurt, but he wouldn't try to force him into something he didn't want.

He smiled, happy that his parents had taken this so well. "How about we head out?" he asked his mother. "We need to get those groceries."

She smiled back. "You're seeing Devon later?"

"Not today, no, but I promised him I would call later." Lorcan wasn't going to break any of the promises he made to Devon. That was one thing he was a hundred percent sure of.

Devon was reading in the living room when he heard Yedley and Justin talking. He didn't want to eavesdrop, but it was hard when he lived with them.

"You need anything else?" Justin asked.

"I forgot to add the butter on the list. Can you please grab a few packs?"

"Of course." There was a moment of silence, and Devon was pretty sure they were kissing. They always seemed to be kissing, and while he found it sweet, it also made him jealous. Could he have that with Lorcan? He wanted to, but he didn't know if he could get over his fear. Some days, he hated himself. He wanted to be able to forgive himself for the mistakes he'd made, to trust Lorcan and have a new life with him. But just when he thought he could manage it, something happened, a thought came out of nowhere, and he freaked out again.

So far, he'd done a good job hiding it from Lorcan, but he knew that the more time they spent together, the better Lorcan would learn to read him. That was what happened when two people got together. Devon realized he shouldn't be ashamed of his past and what had been done to him, but he couldn't help but wonder if Lorcan saw him as weak, or maybe as just not as strong as he should be.

He wasn't weak. He knew that. He was in hiding, but that was because Elroy would hurt him if he found him. Hell, he would hurt not just him, but also the people who had helped him like Justin and Yedley. Devon couldn't allow that to happen.

But would Elroy find him at the grocery store? Probably not. Elroy probably didn't even realize he knew about Gillham. He'd thought Devon was stupid, or at the very least, that he controlled him entirely. He hadn't been careful when he'd talked to his people about Gillham and the pack, which was why Devon knew about it. That was also why Devon had decided to run here. He'd needed a place to hide, and he'd found it. He'd also been able to help the pack, even though he hadn't told them much. Unfortunately, he didn't have anything else to tell them. Some days he wished he did, though. He wanted Elroy to be stopped, and that wouldn't happen easily.

He needed to start living his life. Even if Elroy found him, he might be able to find a way out of whatever the man was planning for him. And if he never found him, well, Devon didn't want to spend the rest of his life hiding just in case.

He swallowed and put his book down. He needed to do

something, to prove to himself and others that he could do this, that he wasn't a coward. No one had said anything like that to him, of course, and he doubted they ever would. They were coddling him, allowing him to hide, and while he'd been relieved in the beginning, it was starting to feel tight. He was hiding because of himself and because he'd thought it was the best thing he could do, but maybe it wasn't.

Elroy was winning. He wasn't in Devon's life anymore, but his presence was, and he still had control over Devon.

It made him angry. He wanted to get rid of Elroy and all the memories he'd shared with the man, and that wouldn't happen if he didn't start living. He needed to do that, to give himself and Lorcan a chance. Otherwise, he would lose his mate, too.

He rose from the couch. His legs felt weak, but he pushed through the feeling and headed to the kitchen, where indeed, Justin and Yedley were kissing. Yedley startled when he noticed him, then laughed, gently pushing Justin away. "We lost track of time." He looked at Justin. "You should go before it gets late."

Justin nodded. "Right. Grocery shopping. I'll be right back." He raised one of Yedley's hands and kissed the back of it.

Devon's heart squeezed at the sight. He was happy for his friends, and he *wanted* them to be happy, but he also he felt jealous. He had a way to stop feeling like this, and he needed to take it.

He was going to, or at the very least, he was going to try. "Justin?" he asked as Justin moved toward the kitchen door.

Justin paused. "Yes?"

"You're going grocery shopping?"

"I am. You need anything?"

Devon shook his head. "I was wondering if I could come with you, though."

Justin blinked at him. "To the grocery store?"

Devon shouldn't be surprised that Justin sounded so unsure and surprised. "Yes. To the grocery store."

"You're sure?"

"I am." Devon wasn't, but it was the best thing he could do right now. He needed to face his fears, and what was better to do that than a grocery shopping run? Elroy wouldn't find him there. He wouldn't go to a grocery store. He never had, even when they'd been together.

Justin beamed. "Of course. You don't even have to ask. Come on."

Devon's heart was racing as they left the house. He looked around, making sure Elroy wasn't hiding in the bushes by the house. He knew it was ridiculous, but it helped him. Elroy was still looking for him, and if this made it easier for him to leave the house, he was going to do it every single time.

Justin noticed it, but he didn't say anything about it. Instead, he went on chattering about what Yedley was planning for dinner and other stuff Devon wasn't really interested in, at least not right now. It already took everything Devon had not to turn around and run back into the house. He was grateful for the chatter, though. It helped him not focus on the fear that was building his chest.

He slightly relaxed once they were in the car and driving away. Justin was still talking, but he paused and looked at Devon briefly. Devon knew what was coming, and he forced himself to smile.

"I'm proud of you," Justin said.

Devon shrugged. "It's the grocery store. I shouldn't be afraid."

"Maybe you shouldn't be, but you being afraid is normal after everything you went through. You don't have to push yourself if you feel uncomfortable."

"I'll never do this if I don't push myself, though."

"Maybe. Just remember that I'm not going anywhere. I won't leave you alone in the store, and if anything happens, you just need to tell me, and I'll get you out of there."

Devon detested that it was needed, but he was also grateful for it. "Thank you," he murmured.

Justin shook his head. "There's nothing to thank me for. You're trying to get your life under control again, and it's a good thing. I know it's hard for you, though."

It was, but Devon finally had for a reason to do it. He had a chance at a second life, at finally being happy. He didn't want to waste it because of Elroy. He didn't want to give the man even more control over him.

Devon's palms were sweaty when they got to the grocery store, but he pushed on. His fingers trembled as he and Justin walked into the shop, and he tried to focus on the stuff on the shelves, handing Justin what he asked for, putting stuff in the cart they'd grabbed at the entrance.

He'd done this before. Doing it again made him remember that, and he slowly relaxed as he slipped into a familiar rhythm.

They were in the cereal aisle when Justin elbowed Devon. "Isn't that your favorite cereal?" he asked.

Devon flushed. It was, but he'd never asked Justin to buy it. He didn't want his friends to take care of him even more than they already were, so he always ate what was put on the table or what was available for him to cook.

"I don't need it," he murmured.

"Maybe not, but it doesn't mean you shouldn't have it. Come on. Grab a box, or even two."

Devon did. It felt weird, especially since he didn't have the money to repay Justin and Yedley, but he didn't know what else to do. The pack was helping them with money since he was considered an informant, but he also realized this couldn't continue forever.

It felt good, though, and he relaxed more as they walked on. He started selecting more products he enjoyed, and every time he looked at Justin in confirmation, Justin smiled at him and nodded.

It was only shopping, and grocery shopping at that, but Devon was having fun. He felt freer than he had in a long time—and happier.

Until he heard someone call his name and he turned around to find Lorcan standing there with an older woman who looked so much like him that it couldn't be anyone but his mother.

Lorcan was stunned to see Devon at the grocery store, but he was also happy. His presence meant that Devon felt comfortable enough to leave Justin's house, and that was a good thing.

A *very* good thing.

The problem was that Devon looked like a deer caught in the headlights. He clearly hadn't expected to meet Lorcan at the grocery store, but then, neither had Lorcan. The fact that Lorcan's mom was there further complicated things, and Lorcan realized he probably shouldn't have called out to Devon when he'd seen him. He'd been so surprised he hadn't thought about it, and now, there they were, staring at each other, with Justin and Lorcan's mom hanging around them looking awkward.

Lorcan wondered what he should do. He didn't want to lie to his mom about who Devon was, but he also didn't want to out Devon as his mate if that wasn't what Devon wanted. He didn't see any other option, though. His mom had heard him call Devon by name, and she knew he was his mate.

Lorcan cleared his throat. "I'm happy to see you," he told Devon.

Devon was looking anywhere but at him, but he nodded. "I'm happy to see you, too."

"So this is my mother," Lorcan said.

Devon looked at her and smiled, but it was tight and nervous. "It's a pleasure to meet you."

"It's a pleasure to meet you too, Devon." Lorcan's mother looked at him. "Lorcan has told me about you."

Devon blinked. "He has?"

"Yes. In fact, he told his father and me about you this morning."

Lorcan's mom was speaking gently, and he knew it was because he'd warned her that Devon had been abused. He was grateful for that, even though Devon still looked like he wanted nothing more than to run away. "I wasn't sure whether or not you'd want me to tell my parents," he began.

Devon shrugged. "I don't see why you shouldn't. This is important. They should know."

"That's what I was thinking. Still, I should have talked to you about it."

Devon hesitated, then shook his head. "You don't have to talk to me about everything. I understand why you wanted to tell your parents about me, and I'm not angry that you did."

He might not be, but he still wasn't comfortable, and Lorcan wasn't sure what to do about it.

"Lorcan told us you were new in town," Lorcan's mom said.

She was staying away from Devon, at least physically, but it was obvious that she was trying to get to know him. The grocery store wasn't the best place for that, especially since Devon had been surprised by their presence. Lorcan wasn't sure what to do about it, though. He couldn't exactly drag his mother away. She probably wouldn't say anything about it, but it would look weird to others, and he didn't know how Devon would react to it. He looked uncomfortable, but he also didn't look like he loathed Lorcan's mother for trying to talk to him.

Lorcan had no idea what to do. He wanted to help Devon, to snatch him away and make sure he was comfortable, but he realized it wasn't something he could do. He needed to leave this up to Devon, but Devon looked like he wasn't sure what to do, either.

"How long are you staying in town?" Lorcan's mom asked.

Devon blinked at her. "I'm not sure. I've never really thought about it."

"I see. And now, you've met Lorcan, which I'm ready to bet complicates things."

"Meeting him means I kind of have to stick around, doesn't it?"

Lorcan's mom looked nonplussed at Devon's answer. "There's no rule that says that you *have* to be with your mate," she said, giving Lorcan an apologetic glance.

Lorcan shook his head. He didn't care if his mother said that to Devon. Hell, he'd been the one to tell Devon in the first place. He didn't want Devon to leave him behind, but if that was what happened, he would deal with it.

"I'm aware of that," Devon said. "I'm not planning on leaving Lorcan, though. I know things can work between us, and I'm going to try. We both are." He looked at Lorcan as he said that, and Lorcan nodded frantically. If they both wanted this, then they needed to make sure it happened, or at the very least, they needed to give it a chance.

"That's good," Lorcan's mom said. "I'm happy I got to meet you. Of course, I wish it weren't at the grocery store because I have so many things to talk with you about."

Devon smiled. It was cautious, but it was a smile, and Lorcan found himself hoping. "You have childhood pictures of Lorcan?" Devon asked.

Lorcan groaned. "Why would you want to see those?"

"I don't know. I guess I just want to see you as a kid. You're cute now, but I imagine you were even cuter when you were a child."

Lorcan's mother laughed. "You're right about that. He wasn't scowling half as much when he was a kid."

"The only reason I'm scowling is that the two of you have ganged up against me," Lorcan muttered. But he was happy. Things were tense and awkward, but Devon and Lorcan's mother were trying, and that was the most important thing.

Devon shuffled his feet. He looked at the floor, and Lorcan's heart hurt for him. He knew Devon wanted more than this. He wanted to be free, but he wouldn't be until Elroy was truly out of his life. Lorcan wanted to do more to help him, but was there anything he could do? He doubted it. This was something Devon needed to realize on his own—a fear he needed to deal with by himself. Lorcan would be there for him if he needed him, but Devon had to do the hard part of the job. Lorcan wished he could do it for him, but that just wasn't possible.

The four of them looked at each other. Justin widened his eyes. He tilted his head at Devon, clearly trying to tell Lorcan something. Lorcan had no idea what he was trying to say.

Justin rolled his eyes, then tilted his head toward Devon again.

Lorcan was starting to think that maybe he could do something for Devon right now. "Did you have anything planned today?" he asked Devon.

Devon startled and looked at him. "What do you mean?"

"What are you doing after grocery shopping? Do you have to cook or something like that? Do you have anything planned?"

Devon looked at Justin, who shrugged, then back at Lorcan. "Not that I know of."

Lorcan wasn't sure Devon would say yes, but he wanted to

try anyway. "How about you come with me?"

Devon blinked. "Where?"

Lorcan should have thought this out better. "I don't know yet, but we can figure it out together."

Devon looked like he wanted to refuse. Lorcan expected him to just that, so he was surprised when Devon slowly nodded. "All right. We can go." He looked at Justin again. "Unless you need me at home? I can help you put the groceries away and cook dinner."

Justin took a step back. "We don't need you to do that," he said. "Yedley and I want you to start living your life, to spend time with your mate."

"But I should help you," Devon insisted.

"You're already helping enough. Don't worry about it, Devon. Go with Lorcan and have fun. Yedley and I can take care of everything."

Devon still didn't look convinced, but Lorcan found himself praying that he would say yes. He understood where Devon was coming from and why he wanted to help Justin and Yedley, but he wanted some time with his mate, and he suspected that Devon needed a moment to relax after what had just happened.

Devon had no idea what was going on, but he did know that he wanted to leave the grocery store. He felt guilty about it. He'd told Justin that he would help, but instead, he was running away like a coward—again. But he hadn't planned on meeting Lorcan's mother today, and the thought that he'd talked to her made him panic. He didn't want either Lorcan or his mother to realize that, though. They were trying to be nice, and Devon didn't have a reason to feel the way he did.

But he did feel that way, and he couldn't change that. When Lorcan offered him his hand, he took it and allowed his mate to drag him outside. He remembered to say goodbye at the last second, turning and waving. Justin waved back, and Devon saw Lorcan's mother lean closer to him, asking him something. Then Lorcan was pulling him around the aisle, and they were gone from sight.

Devon followed his mate until they were out of the grocery store. Then, once in the parking lot, he stopped and forced Lorcan to stop, too. "Where are we going?" he asked.

Lorcan shrugged. "I have no idea. We can take a walk, though. I'm sure it will make you feel more comfortable than being in there with my mother."

Devon didn't know how to answer that. He wanted to take a walk with Lorcan. They hadn't been supposed to see each other today, but now they were together, and he didn't want it to end. He was also wary, though. He disliked feeling that way, but his first instinct was to make sure they stayed in a public place so Lorcan couldn't hurt him.

He knew Lorcan wouldn't. They'd been alone before, and nothing had happened. But his brain was all jumbled, and his heart was still racing in his chest. It hadn't stopped, not since the moment he'd heard his name in the grocery store.

Devon forced himself to stop panicking. It was hard, but if he focused on what was happening instead of what his brain was telling him, it might happen, and that made it easier.

He was with Lorcan. He was safe. No matter what his heart and brain were telling him, he knew that. Lorcan wouldn't hurt him. They were outside of the grocery store and headed somewhere because Lorcan wanted Devon to have space. He'd realized Devon was uncomfortable with his mother, and he was trying to help. Lorcan was *always* trying to help, and Devon needed to keep that in mind.

He sucked in a breath. "All right. Let's go for a walk." He hesitated. "Unless your mother needs your help."

Lorcan froze. "Shit. I forgot I drove her here."

"We don't have to go anywhere," Devon answered even though now that he'd started thinking about the walk, he wanted to go.

Lorcan shook his head. "I can run inside to give her my car keys, or we can just stick around until they're both done with grocery shopping. Just tell me what you want."

Devon had no idea what he wanted, which was a problem. He looked around. Lorcan couldn't go far, because his mother would need him to go home, but the park was right there, close enough that they could sit on a bench and wait for Justin and Lorcan's mother.

Devon swallowed. "The park?" he asked.

Lorcan beamed at him. "That's an excellent idea. I know a quiet area. We can go there. I'll just text my mother and Justin so they don't wonder where we've gone."

Devon nodded. He was grateful Lorcan was thinking of everything. He detested feeling like he was letting life push and pull him around, but right now, he couldn't deal with anything more.

He felt like an idiot. He hadn't expected to see Lorcan and his mother today, but that didn't mean he had to freak out the way he had. Hopefully, he'd managed to hide it, at least for a while. Lorcan's mother hadn't seemed to think he was crazy, so that was a plus. He also hadn't really talked to her, though, and he couldn't help but wonder what she thought of him as her son's mate. Would she demand Lorcan break up with Devon if he didn't start behaving normally? Did she think he was weird and not good enough for her son?

"You're thinking way too hard for a walk in the park," Lorcan said, interrupting Devon's thoughts.

Devon looked at him. They were still holding hands, and it made Devon feel safer. That was strange, since until a few minutes earlier Devon's brain had been terrified Lorcan would hurt him, but he'd stopped trying to find logic in his thoughts and feelings. They didn't have it, not most of the time. "I was thinking about your mother," he said.

Lorcan grimaced. "I'm going to admit that I'm not happy you're thinking about my mother when you're on a date with me."

Devon's eyes widened. "We're on a date?"

"I don't know. Why not? We're together, alone. It could be a date if we want it to be one. I know we've already agreed on Saturday, but this could be just a short coffee date or something like that."

"Does that mean the coffee we had together the other day was a date, too?" Devon wouldn't mind that. It would certainly help him freak out less about going on a first date with Lorcan if they'd already had that first date.

"I know. We don't have to think about this or any other time we spend together as a date. We can just be together, and that's it. What do you think?"

"I'd like that." Not thinking about what they were doing as a date took a lot of the expectations away, and it was easier to breathe.

He followed Lorcan until Lorcan found a bench. He had taken Devon to a quiet part of the park just like he'd said, and while a few people were walking around, it was mostly quiet, no doubt thanks to the fact that it was the middle of the day and people were at work. They sat on the bench, and Devon looked at the small pond. He could see butterflies exploring the bushes and flowers, a few bees, and even fish. There was a duck, his butt poking out of a bunch of aquatic plants.

It was peaceful. It felt like paradise, and Devon found himself relaxing even though he didn't mean to. He didn't fear Lorcan. He didn't think he'd ever truly feared his mate, but sometimes, panic was the first thing to make him act. The thoughts came later, and the last thing he wanted was to hurt Lorcan by reacting instinctively around him. He knew Lorcan would understand, but he shouldn't have to. He shouldn't have to see his mate shy away from him—afraid he was going to hurt him.

He took a deep breath. He wanted to say something, to apologize for the way he'd been behaving, but Lorcan beat him to it.

"I'm sorry for making you uncomfortable," he said. He was looking at the pond, but he was still holding Devon's hand, and Devon clung to it as a lifeline.

"You don't have to apologize. You didn't know I was going to be at the grocery store. I didn't know I was going to be there until I saw Justin was leaving the house."

Lorcan looked at Devon. "You asked to go with him?"

"I did." Devon wasn't sure what had possessed him to do it, and he knew he should probably regret it considering everything that had happened, but he didn't. Going with Justin to the grocery store had given him this moment with Lorcan, and it was what he wanted. He wanted *more*, even though he wasn't sure how to ask for it. He supposed it would come, with time. In the meantime, he could focus on what they already had.

"My mom didn't mean anything, you know. She was trying to make you feel at ease. I told her what happened to you, although I didn't go into details. I wanted her and my father to understand why I wasn't introducing you to them yet."

Devon took a moment to think about it. "I'm not angry because you told them about me."

"Are you sure?"

"I am. I'm ashamed of what happened, but I realize that some people need to know, especially when it comes to your family. I can only imagine how she would have reacted at meeting me if you hadn't told her what happened, and I don't think I would have been able to explain, so thank you."

"You don't have to thank me or to feel ashamed of what

Elroy did. You had no fault in that."

"Of course I did. I allowed him to do all of that."

Lorcan shook his head. "You didn't allow him to do anything. You did what you had to do to survive, and in my book, that means you're fucking brave. Not a lot of people would have been, and besides, you found a way to live through it. You *left*, and you're safe now. And if I know you, the main reason you left Elroy behind was that you wanted to save Gillham, not yourself."

Lorcan was rambling and his voice sounded heated, but it wasn't directed at Devon. Devon's heart warmed—his mate was defending him.

Maybe Lorcan was right. Maybe Devon *had* been courageous when he'd left Elroy behind. None of that mattered right now, though. What *did* matter was that Lorcan was defending him, and Devon couldn't resist anymore.

He surprised even himself when he reached for Lorcan and kissed the corner of his lips. Lorcan stopped talking and blinked at Devon, but Devon didn't move back, even though his heart was racing and he felt the need to run.

He didn't *have* to run, though. He was with his mate, and he was safe.

"You kissed me," Lorcan said.

Devon laughed. He felt lighter, happier. "I did."

"Can you kiss me again?"

"I can." And Devon did. This was yet another step forward for him, and he was more than happy to give in to the need and want to kiss his mate.

CHAPTER FIVE

Things were going well, or at least, it felt like they were. Lorcan couldn't deny he was still slightly apprehensive when he thought about his life with Devon, but Devon was much more relaxed since their walk in the park. They'd been talking and texting, and tonight was the night of their first date. Or maybe it wasn't the first. It didn't matter. As long as Lorcan could be with Devon and talk to him, he was more than happy to call it whatever Devon wanted.

And they'd kissed. Well, Devon had kissed Lorcan. Lorcan hadn't expected it, and he wished they'd had more time, but after only about fifteen minutes, Justin and Lorcan's mom had come out of the grocery store, and Devon and Lorcan had gone their separate ways. Lorcan wished they hadn't had to, but he hoped Devon was finally seeing what Lorcan had been saying all along. They belonged together, and Lorcan would never hurt him.

Lorcan had the feeling that Devon was finally getting used to having him in his life. He knew he couldn't push, no matter how much he wanted to. That would send Devon running, and that was the last thing Lorcan wanted. What he wanted was for Devon to be happy, to feel comfortable with him. Devon's feelings were the only thing that mattered, and Lorcan was being incredibly careful with them. Still, he couldn't help that he hadn't stopped smiling since their date at the park, to the point that he was irritating his friends.

His phone rang, and he wasn't surprised to see it was his mom. They hadn't talked much on their way back home after grocery shopping the other day, but she'd been vibrating with unasked questions. Lorcan hadn't told her to ask, mostly because he hadn't known how to answer yet. He still wasn't sure, but he still answered the phone. "Mom."

"Okay. I gave you time, but you haven't called me yet. I need to know what happened with Devon at the park," she said.

Lorcan relaxed. He hadn't even realized he was tense, but he wasn't surprised. When his parents called, he was always afraid it was to tell them they'd been attacked, that they were hurt. He knew it was ridiculous, but he couldn't help it.

He leaned back on his bed. "What do you want to know?"

She huffed. "What happened at the park?" she repeated. "Did you and Devon talk? What did he say? Was he angry because I was there? Did I offend him in any way or scare him?"

Lorcan waited until the torrent of questions was over, then he said, "He wasn't angry with you, Mom. You don't have to worry about that."

"How am I not supposed to worry about it? I don't want my son-in-law to be terrified of me because I couldn't keep my mouth shut."

Hearing the words *son-in-law* coming in his mom's voice made something flutter in Lorcan's chest. "We're not quite at the son-in-law stage yet," he pointed out.

"Hush. You might not be bonded, but it doesn't change the fact that Devon is your mate. Whether or not you end up together, that fact will never change, and he'll always be my son-in-law. He'll always have a home with me and your father."

That touched Lorcan more than he could say. He needed Devon to be aware of that, to know that whatever happened, he would always have a family. Devon didn't need one, of course, since he had Justin and Yedley, and probably other people he didn't realize were his friends. But this was important. This was Lorcan's parents accepting Devon in their life, whether or not Devon wanted to be with Lorcan. It would be hell if that was what happened, but Lorcan would learn to deal with it. He didn't have to like it to be able to do that.

"I'll let him know," he said quietly.

There was a moment of silence, then his mom asked, "Can you tell me more about his ex-boyfriend?"

"What do you want to know?" Devon hadn't seemed angry that Lorcan had told his parents about what had happened to him. He doubted that giving his mom more details would be a problem for him, but he didn't want to blurt everything out.

"Is that man from Gillham? Is he still a danger to Devon?"

There was a fierceness in her voice, and Lorcan knew she would defend Devon as she would Lorcan or Liam. He had to clear his throat before he could answer. Emotion choked him, and he didn't want his mom to realize how much this meant to him, even though she probably already knew. "He's not from here. When Devon ran away, he came to Gillham, hoping his ex wouldn't think of looking for him here."

"Of course he wouldn't. Gillham is a small town."

"You don't get it, Mom. You know about Elroy?"

"You mean the man who's planning to attack Gillham?"

"Him. *He's* Devon's ex. One of the reasons Devon ran to Gillham was that he wanted us to know Elroy was planning something."

"My God. Poor boy. He really went through hell and back, didn't he?"

"I think so. He hasn't given me many details, and I doubt he's planning to. He doesn't like to talk about it."

"I'm not surprised. Who would like to talk about something like this?"

"But he's told us that Elroy abused him, and it took a lot of courage from him to leave the man and come here. He knew Elroy might catch him at any moment, and it still might happen. Yet he understood Gillham was in danger, and he wanted to save us. He wanted to help."

"He's so brave."

Lorcan agreed. He knew Devon didn't feel that way, but that didn't matter. Eventually, he would realize that Lorcan and his mother were right.

He might have run away, but that didn't make him weak. Actually, considering the circumstances, it made him brave. It made him strong, strong enough to risk his life to let the people of Gillham know they were in danger.

"You're taking care of him, aren't you?" Lorcan's mother asked.

"As much as I can. As much as he allows me to." But Lorcan was starting to realize that Devon was fiercely independent. He hadn't been allowed to be that way for a long time, and now that he was, he wanted things to go his way. Still, he was making a place in his life for Lorcan, and that was everything Lorcan could hope for. He knew he needed to give Devon the time and space to figure himself out. His personality had been stomped down by Elroy, and he'd lost his way. This was his chance to find himself again, to start a new life. Hopefully, Lorcan would be in it, and they would be together.

"You have a date tonight, don't you?" his mom asked.

Lorcan wasn't surprised she remembered. "We do."

"Are you nervous?"

Lorcan huffed. "Why are we talking about this?" They'd never talked about his dates before, although that probably was because he'd never brought a boyfriend home. He'd come close a few times, but none of his exes had been as important as Devon was.

"Because I worry about you and Devon. I want the two of you to be happy."

"We're working toward that, Mom. I can't rush things. It would make him bolt, and I can't allow that to happen. I want him in my life."

"You're doing the right thing. I know that when you meet your mate, you only want to push ahead, to start living your life together. It's what your father and I did. But Devon is different. None of us have gone through what he's going through, and you need to give him time."

Lorcan didn't point out that was what he was trying to do. It was obvious his mom was worried about Devon, and he loved that. He loved that she already cared, even though they'd only met once.

"I'll take care of him," he promised.

"I know. I love you, Lorcan. And please. Tell Devon that he's always welcome here."

"I will." Lorcan had no idea what was going to happen, how his date with Devon would end, but he was more optimistic than he'd been until recently. Things between them were looking better and better. Maybe they really could do this. Maybe they could be together and be happy.

Devon had to cancel the date. It didn't matter that he and Lorcan were working things out or that this was actually their third date, Devon was still nervous, and he couldn't do it. He couldn't go out there, where everyone could see him — where Elroy might find him. He couldn't face Lorcan. He wanted to be with him, but this was too much. He had to stop this, and he had to do it before Lorcan arrived.

He stopped pacing his bedroom and rubbed his hands on his thighs. His cell phone was on his bed, and he eyed it, knowing he needed to call Lorcan to explain. Lorcan would understand, and it almost made Devon feel worse. Lorcan was such an understanding man, and he would know why

Devon wanted to stay home. He wouldn't push, wouldn't ask for an explanation. He would be disappointed, but he would do whatever Devon needed, and Devon abhorred it. He wanted Lorcan to yell at him. He wanted Lorcan to be angry.

He sighed. He knew he wanted that because it would give him a reason to put even more space between them. It would be easier for him to shield his heart and to make sure he wouldn't get hurt again.

But instead, Lorcan would *understand*, and Devon would feel like shit.

"Something tells me this isn't going well," Yedley said from the open bedroom door.

Devon should have closed it, but he didn't like it when doors were closed. It made him feel like a prisoner again.

He looked at his friend, unsure of how to answer. "I can't do this," he finally said.

Yedley frowned and stepped in. He hovered there until Devon waved at him to walk in, and once he did, and sat on the bed, watching Devon as he started pacing again.

"What's going on?" Yedley asked.

"I can't do this," Devon repeated. "I can't go on this date."

"Why?"

"I'm afraid someone will see us. What if Elroy sent someone to Gillham and they see me? They'll recognize me and let him know I'm here. Then he'll attack and take me back."

Yedley shook his head. "Even if he did send someone, and even if they do recognize you, we already know he's planning to attack. It won't change anything whether or not he knows you're here."

"But he'll try to force me to go back." And Devon *couldn't* go back. He couldn't go through this again.

"Is that the only reason you're freaking out?"

Devon didn't know anymore. Maybe it was, maybe it wasn't. "I'm scared."

81

"I know Lorcan didn't do anything to scare you, so it's something else."

"He's been nothing but understanding and gentle and *good*. But what if in the end he's like Elroy? Elroy was like that, too. He was nice—until he wasn't."

"Lorcan isn't like Elroy."

Devon knew that. He knew for sure that Lorcan wouldn't hurt him, but he couldn't stop. Panic was clinging to him like a shield, a shell that was impossible to break. He sucked in a breath. "I need to call Lorcan to tell him I can't do this."

"Wait," Yedley said, stopping Devon as he reached for his phone.

Devon froze. If there was even one chance he could go on the date, he wanted to take it. He wanted to stop Elroy from having such an influence on him. He wanted to be happy and let go of the past and the memories. He didn't know if Yedley had a way to make that happen, but he was going to listen to him.

Yedley patted the mattress next to him. "Sit down."

Devon obeyed. He suspected he already knew what Yedley was going to say, but maybe hearing it a second time would help.

"Lorcan is a good man," he said.

Devon nodded. He didn't say anything. He didn't have to.

"He won't hurt you. But if he does, you can come to Justin or me, and we'll kick his ass. Hell, you can go to any of his team members, and the same will happen. They won't allow Lorcan or anyone to hurt you. You're not alone anymore. You won't have to run if something happens, not like you had to with Elroy, and that means something. You have a family now, and we'll always be there for you, even if it means going against Lorcan. Hell, if he hurts you, he'll probably get booted out of the enforcers. He won't be welcome in Gillham any-more."

Devon didn't want that to happen. "I know all of that," he murmured.

"Then what's wrong? Is it the anxiety? You're letting it take over?"

Devon nodded. "Even though rationally, I know all of this, I can't help but wonder *what if*? It's not just that I'm afraid Lorcan would hurt me, because I know he won't. But what if someone recognizes me? What if Elroy comes after me? What if instead of attacking Gillham, he sneaks in and takes me away? Maybe I should stay home. It would be safer for everyone, especially me and Lorcan."

Yedley didn't answer right away. Instead, he sucked on his lower lip, taking his time. Devon was grateful. It gave him a moment to breathe in and out and try to calm his racing heart.

"I know you want to be free of Elroy," he started.

"Of course I want to be free of him. But it's never going to happen." Devon was starting to realize that, and he didn't know what to do about it.

"You're strong. You're one of the strongest people I've ever met, and my best friend was in a lab for years. But you're letting Elroy control your life even now that he's not in it. I understand why you're afraid, and that you might not be wrong when you say that he's going to come looking for you. But you're safe. You live with me and Justin, and you have friends. You're not alone anymore, and no one is going to allow anyone to put their hands on you, least of all Elroy. You managed to warn the pack about what was going to happen, and they ramped up security, both in pack territory and Gillham. Yes, someone might see you and tell Elroy, but I doubt he'll manage to get to you."

There was no way to know for sure. That was a problem. Even though Devon wanted to go on that date, wanted to be happy with Lorcan and get Elroy out of his life, he didn't know if he could. Elroy was a mean person, a man who wouldn't stop for anything to get what he wanted — and what he wanted was Devon, unfortunately.

The doorbell rang, making Devon jump. He looked at Yedley with wide eyes. "It's too late. I can't call him to cancel the date," he whispered.

Yedley smiled at him and patted his knee. "Then don't. Go downstairs and talk to him. Explain to him that you're afraid and that you don't want to go on the date. Hell, ask him if he wants to come in. You know Justin and I won't mind."

Devon was tempted to do just that, but Yedley was right. Devon was allowing Elroy to take over, to influence his life even though he was away from the man. He shouldn't do that.

He swallowed. "I can do this," he said.

Yedley smiled. "I know you can. And if anything happens, Justin and I are just a phone call away."

Devon nodded and rose from the bed. He took a deep breath, then another, and grabbed his phone from the bed. Then he headed downstairs to his mate.

Lorcan looked good enough to eat. Devon was surprised he felt that way, since the last time he'd had sex, it had been with Elroy, and since then, he hadn't even felt the desire to do it. He'd thought Elroy had taken that away from him, too, but instead, his body burned at the sight of his mate waiting for him on the porch, especially when Lorcan looked up and smiled at him. Devon couldn't help but smile back, and some of the panic softened. He could still feel it, gripping his stomach, telling him to run, but he knew he could do this.

"Hi," he said, unsure what else to say.

"Hi. You look gorgeous," Lorcan answered.

Devon shuffled his feet. "So do you." He swallowed. "Where are we going?"

"Do you trust me?"

"Of course I do," Devon said before he could think better

of it. And he did. He did trust Lorcan.

"Let's go, then," Lorcan said, offering Devon his hand.

Devon took it.

Lorcan knew something was wrong when he picked Devon up. He could see it in Devon's expression, in the tightness around his eyes, in the little frown on his lips. But he'd smiled when he saw Lorcan, and Lorcan prayed everything would be okay. He never wanted Devon to do something he wasn't ready for, and that included going on a date with him.

They climbed into the car, and Lorcan paused. "Are you sure you're up to this?" he asked, even though he was afraid of the answer.

Devon took a moment, and Lorcan held his breath. "I'll be fine," Devon finally said, his voice soft.

"I don't want you to be *fine*. I want you to feel comfortable. I want you to be happy. If you don't feel ready to do this, we can just stay here, or you can stay and I can go home, and we'll try again another time."

Devon shook his head. "I want to do this. Right now, there's nothing I want more. I want to leave my whole life behind. I want to focus on my future, and *you* are my future."

Those words made Lorcan feel wobbly. He'd been feeling the same way toward Devon for a while now, but he hadn't realized Devon shared those feelings. "I want to be your future, too."

Devon smiled. "Then be it. Come on. Show me what you had in mind."

It had been hard to decide what to do. Lorcan knew Devon pretty well by now, and he was aware of the fact that Devon would be uncomfortable in a place with a lot of people. That meant that for their first date, he had to find a relatively calm place and with few people, but not so much that he and

Devon would be alone. That would freak Devon out, too, because then Lorcan might be able to hurt him and no one would intervene.

"I hope you like Chinese food," Lorcan said.

Devon blinked. "Chinese food?"

"It's my favorite restaurant. It's never full, so you don't have to worry about that, but we won't be alone. You'll be able to relax and eat good food."

Devon nodded and bit his lower lip. "I hate that you had to think of that," he confessed.

"Think of what? That I want you to be comfortable?"

"That I might not want to be alone with you."

"That's fine. I'm not offended. I know you can't help it."

"Maybe not, but I hate it. I want to be alone with you. I want us to be a real couple."

"We are a real couple as long as we want to be one."

"Shouldn't we have at least sex first? I mean, that's what couples do."

Lorcan gritted his teeth. "We can have sex, sure. We don't *have* to, though. Not having sex doesn't mean we're not a couple. How do you think asexual people make things work?"

"I hadn't thought about that. I guess that since I had sex with my boyfriends, I felt it was a requirement."

Lorcan wasn't surprised. He didn't know if Devon's exes were all like Elroy, but even if they weren't, sex was important for a lot of people. "It's not. Nothing is a requirement in a relationship. If you want us to be a couple and I do, too, then that's what we are. We'll decide together what we want from this relationship, okay?"

Lorcan could feel Devon's gaze on him, and he was grateful he was able to focus on driving. "What if I *want* to have sex with you?" Devon asked softly.

Lorcan almost drove the car off the road. "We'll get there," he said, his heart racing.

"How can you be sure of that? You know how I am. How do you think I'm going to react if we're alone in a room? It's not like we can have sex with someone there watching us."

When Lorcan looked over, Devon's cheeks were flushed. "We don't have to do it if you're uncomfortable. Look, Devon. We don't have to make any kind of decision right now. We can go on this date and see where things go."

"Don't you want to have sex with me?"

It was obvious from Devon's tone that he expected a rejection, and he couldn't have been more wrong. "I do want to have sex with you. I've wanted it since I saw you that first day, but I can restrain myself. I don't have a problem if you never want to have sex with me. I'm falling in love with you regardless, and that's not going to change. So yes. I do want to make love to you, but I'm never going to push you for something you're not ready for. I want you to want it as much as I do, and we won't do anything until that's the case."

Devon looked like he wasn't sure what to think, and Lorcan was grateful he didn't ask anything. He needed a moment to get over the effect Devon's words had on him. He focused on the road for a bit, until they got to the restaurant. He was relieved to see that it was half-empty, just as usual, and that the hostess gave them a table in the back. They were isolated, but not so much that people couldn't see them, and Lorcan was relieved to see Devon relax once he realized that and understood he was safe.

Lorcan loathed that his mate didn't feel safe with him, but that would change. Devon had a lot to overcome, and that included his relationship with an abuser. Lorcan was going to show him what people in love were like, what they did for each other, but at his own pace, not at Lorcan's.

"It's good," Devon said as he bit into a spring roll. He was smiling and looked at peace.

That made Lorcan's heart soften. He wanted Devon to

always smile. He knew it wasn't possible, but his heart demanded it. "I love this place. I discovered it a few weeks after it opened, and I've been coming ever since. I usually come with my brother, though."

"Not with your friends?"

Lorcan shrugged. "Depends on who. A few don't like Chinese food, which is a pity because it's delicious. But yeah. I usually come with people I care about — friends, family members, you know."

Devon cocked his head. "Is that an underhanded way of telling me you care about me?"

"I thought you already knew I did."

Devon looked away, but he was smiling. "You're right. I know you care about me," he said, his voice barely louder than a whisper.

Still, the words went straight to Lorcan's heart. "More than you can understand," he confessed.

"I think I *can* understand," Devon answered, and they stared at each other, both of them smiling.

The moment broke when the waitress came around with their rice dishes, but that was okay. If things went the way Lorcan wanted them to, they would have plenty of moments in the future.

All in all, Lorcan thought the date was going well. Devon relaxed, and as they filled themselves with Chinese food, he started chatting about his sister and his time in foster care. Not all of it was happy, but Lorcan listened to whatever Devon had to say. He couldn't do anything for what had happened in Devon's past. What he *could* do was make sure that Devon's future was as happy as possible, and he had all intention of doing just that.

Things were slightly awkward every so often. Sometimes, the conversation dropped, and they looked at each other, both unsure what to say. They managed to get out of those moments easily enough, though, usually because Lorcan found something else to talk about. Devon was adorably flustered, his cheeks pinking more and more as the time passed even though he wasn't drinking alcohol. This was the real Devon—the one fear didn't rule, the one who should have stayed this way and who had been temporarily ruined by Elroy. But Lorcan would make sure the real Devon had all the time and space he needed to come back. He wanted Devon to be happy, and he thought he was doing a good job.

Things became even more awkward as Lorcan drove Devon back home. He was pretty sure they were both thinking about the same thing—was Lorcan going to kiss Devon goodnight? Lorcan wanted to. Hell, if it was up to him, he would never stop kissing Devon. Now that he'd had a taste, he was addicted, but in the best of ways. He didn't want to push Devon too fast, too hard, though, so once they were on the porch, both of them shuffling their feet like two teenagers, he gestured at the car. "I should let you get some sleep," he said.

Devon nodded. "I'm sure you have work tomorrow, so yes, it's probably better if you go." He hesitated. "I had a good time," he added.

Lorcan couldn't help but smile. "I had a good time, too."

"The food was great, and being with you, well, it makes me happy."

"Good." That was what Lorcan wanted.

"So I guess this is it?" Devon asked.

Lorcan decided that maybe he should push a little bit. After all, Devon had initiated their first kiss. Maybe he should be the one to take that step this time. "Can I kiss you?" he asked before he could overthink it.

Devon's cheeks flushed, and Lorcan was grateful to the porch light that allowed him to see it. "Please. I didn't want to ask in case you didn't want to, but I really want to kiss you."

So Lorcan did. He leaned forward, resisting the urge to wrap himself around Devon. He wanted nothing more, but he knew it would make Devon feel restrained. Instead of focusing on that, he rubbed their lips together, and Devon sighed happily. He opened his mouth, and Lorcan slipped his tongue inside, smiling when Devon groaned and pushed himself closer.

Lorcan was careful not to let things go too far. Devon might feel like he wanted that right now, but he could regret it later, once he had time to think about it, and Lorcan didn't want that. When they were together, once they had sex, he never wanted Devon to regret any of it.

They were both breathing hard by the time they separated. Lorcan had to resist the urge to lean forward again, to kiss Devon a second time, a third, a fourth. Instead, he took a step back and rubbed his face. "I really should go before I change my mind and decide to stay," he said.

Devon laughed. "I guess it would be better, yes. I'll see you tomorrow?"

"Of course. I'll text you later to tell you I'm home, and we can decide when and where."

Lorcan waited until Devon had turned away and entered the house to go back to his car. He was walking on clouds, feeling happier than he ever had. He knew he was going to have to defend that happiness, but he was ready to do just that. If Elroy wanted a fight, then he would get one.

Devon sighed happily as he closed the door and leaned against it. He couldn't believe he'd almost not gone on that date. He was relieved he had now, and he wanted to dismiss the fear entirely.

He almost did. But even though he wasn't afraid of Lorcan

anymore — and when he thought rationally about it — he knew his other fears were still there, and that they were warranted. Someone could have seen them and would report to Elroy, and then Elroy would come to get him.

But Devon didn't want to allow Elroy to ruin their date. It had been perfect, the best date Devon had ever been on, and he wanted to do it again and again. He wanted Lorcan in his life and for him to never leave.

He knew he looked like an idiot as he smiled all the way to his bedroom. Justin and Yedley were in the living room, cuddled on the couch watching TV, and Yedley looked up when he heard the door. Devon waved at him, and he was sure Yedley knew from his smile that everything had gone well. He didn't move from the couch. Instead, he was smiling and waving back, and Devon headed upstairs. He needed some time to wrap his mind around everything that had just happened.

He knew Lorcan wasn't perfect. No one was. And even though Lorcan was his mate, he realized that the relationship with him would take work. For the first time in forever, though, it felt good to think about it. It didn't spark fear in him — didn't make him want to run away. He was ready to work to be happy, and he knew that if he had Lorcan in his life, it would be worth it.

He walked into his bedroom, closed the door, and flopped onto his bed. He was still smiling, and he doubted he would stop anytime soon. *God.* Now that he was alone, he realized he hadn't wanted to leave Lorcan. Maybe he should have tried to convince his mate to stay or something. He wasn't sure he was ready for sex, but he wanted it, much more than usual. He wanted to become one with his mate, and he wanted it to happen soon. The last man who had touched him that way had been Elroy, and Devon could still remember the pain. He never wanted to go through that again, but Lorcan was different, and knowing that helped Devon get over the fear. It wasn't perfect, of course. Elroy had never raped Devon, but that didn't mean Devon had willingly had sex with him. He'd done it because he knew that things would get worse for him if he didn't, but now, he *wanted* it. He almost couldn't recognize himself.

He took his phone out of his jeans pocket, wanting to have it close when Lorcan texted him. Even though they'd just left each other, he already missed his mate. He smiled when he saw he had a text message, but instead of being from Lorcan, it was from Cedric, and the words made Devon shoot up in a sitting position.

Call me ASAP.

Devon's heart beat faster at the thought that something had happened to his friend. He should have known better than to think his life was going to be okay now. He was happy, but Cedric was still there, and he was still hurting.

Devon took his other phone with trembling hands. He probably shouldn't have given Cedric his new number, but he'd wanted his friend to be able to reach him at any moment. He hoped it hadn't been a mistake.

He turned the old phone on, and there was another text from Cedric. He still wanted Devon to call him, so Devon did, even though his heart was racing so hard that he wasn't sure he would be able to hear anything.

"Cedric?" he asked as soon as someone answered.

It wasn't Cedric.

"I've been looking for you," Elroy drawled.

Devon scrambled off the bed, pushing himself into the space between the bed and the wall. He fell on the floor and pressed his back against the wall even though he knew Elroy couldn't see him. He wasn't here. He wasn't in the bedroom or in the house, and he probably wasn't in Gillham since he had Cedric's phone. "Where's Cedric?" Devon asked. It was hard to push the words through his fear, but he needed to know what had happened to his friend.

"Cedric? You mean your little friend?" There was a pause, then someone screamed, and Devon was sure it was Cedric.

Devon sobbed. "Stop hurting him!"

"Why should I? Did he help you run away, pet?"

"He had nothing to do with it. I ran away on my own." And it was the truth. He'd asked Cedric to go with him, but Cedric had been too afraid. He'd kept Devon's secret, though, and Devon knew Elroy wouldn't take it well if he found out.

"And you think I'm going to believe that? Where are you?" Devon wasn't about to answer. It would only make Elroy angrier, and he would come. He would leave fear and pain and death in his path, and Devon couldn't allow that to happen. "Tell me where you are. I'll come to you," he said before he could think better of it.

It was the last thing he wanted. He never wanted to see Elroy again, let alone go to him. But Cedric was in pain. He was probably being tortured, and he risked being killed. Devon couldn't allow that to happen. Even though they hadn't seen each other for in a while, Cedric was still his friend, and Devon needed to protect him.

"If I'd known it was that easy, I would have tortured your little friend sooner," Elroy said. "You know where I am. I expect you to be back by the end of the evening."

"By the morning. I need to do a few things before I come." There was a pause, and Devon knew he was pushing, maybe too much. Elroy had never been a tolerant man.

Devon was surprised when he agreed. "All right. I expect you by the morning, then." He paused. "But don't think I'm going to let you come back without punishing you. You ran away from me, pet. You're going to pay for that."

Devon had known that since he'd left, so he wasn't surprised by Elroy's words. "I know," he said softly.

"And while I wait for you, I'm going to punish your

friend."

Devon opened his mouth to protest, but Elroy had already hung up.

Devon dropped the phone and closed his eyes. The situation was the worst he could have imagined. Not only was he going back to Elroy, but Elroy was torturing his friend. He was hurting Cedric because of him.

Maybe Devon shouldn't have left Elroy. Maybe he should have stayed with him until the man killed him. Instead, he'd only thought of himself, and he'd run away, leaving Cedric with the Beasts and Elroy.

And now Cedric was paying for it.

Devon reached up and dried the tears from his cheeks. Elroy was expecting him by morning. He was going to continue torturing Cedric, whatever Devon said or did. Even if Devon found him in the next five minutes, Elroy wasn't going to stop. He never did. As much as Devon hated it, it gave him some time.

He wanted a last memory with Lorcan, even though he knew it would piss off Elroy. If this was the last time he would see Lorcan, then he had to do this.

He swallowed and got to his feet. His knees felt like jelly, but he knew he could do this. He straightened, went to the bathroom to wash his face, then headed back downstairs. Yedley and Justin were still on the couch, and when Devon cleared his throat, they both looked up. Justin frowned and tried to get to his feet, but Devon shook his head and forced himself to smile. "I was just wondering if Yedley could shimmer me to Lorcan."

"Is something wrong?" Justin asked.

"No. It's just that I, you know—I thought better about it, and I realized that I wanted to spend the night with him." Devon's cheeks felt like fire, but this was what he wanted. It was what he *needed*—the last memories he would have with

Lorcan. If Elroy didn't kill him, he would do it himself. He couldn't live that life again, not after he'd known what happiness was.

Yedley smiled and got to his feet. "That's how it is, huh?"

Devon hoped the smile on his lips was believable. "You know. We talked, and I realized he truly wants what's best for me."

"Come on. I'll shimmer you," Yedley offered him his hand, and Devon took it.

It was only a few seconds before they were standing in front of the enforcers' building. Yedley smiled at Devon, made sure he was okay, then shimmered away, leaving Devon there. Devon sucked in a breath, then knocked on the door.

The woman who opened gave him directions to Lorcan's bedroom, and he found it easily. Once he was standing in front of the door, he took another deep breath, raised his hand, and knocked.

He couldn't live without having at least this. The rest of his life was going to be painful, and he needed the memories to get through it.

Lorcan's eyes went wide when he opened the door. He opened his mouth, probably to ask what was going on, but Devon didn't let him. Instead, he pushed himself forward and fell onto Lorcan, reaching out for him and pulling him down to kiss him. Lorcan made a strangled sound, but he went along with it, wrapping his arms around Devon and pulling him inside the bedroom, slamming the door behind them.

This was what Devon wanted. It was what he needed, and for once, he was going to get it.

He reached for Lorcan's jeans, wanting to push them off. His fingers felt stiff, though, and he couldn't get the button to slip out of the hole, no matter how many times he tried. He huffed, frustrated, and stopped kissing Lorcan to focus on it, but Lorcan took both his hands and squeezed.

"What's going on?" he asked.

Devon shook his head. He couldn't answer that question. He knew he should tell Lorcan about Cedric and Elroy. Lorcan would take charge, contact his team and his boss, and they'd try to save Cedric.

Devon couldn't risk it. The enforcers were protecting the town and pack territory. He couldn't distract them, not when he could solve this on his own. He'd been a coward until now, but no more.

"Devon?"

Devon shook his head. "Nothing."

"This doesn't look like nothing to me," Lorcan said, gently squeezing Devon's hands.

"I just—I've had enough of being afraid. I want you. You want me. I want to bond with you." He was afraid to look at Lorcan, afraid of what he would see in his gaze and his expression.

"I want the same thing, but are you sure? I don't want you to regret it."

Lorcan couldn't understand, and Devon couldn't explain. The only thing he could do was nod. "I'm sure. I don't want to be afraid anymore, Lorcan. I've been terrified for too long, and even now, I can't let go. But I want to. I trust you. There's no one else I trust more, and I don't want to allow fear to keep me back. You've been incredibly patient with me, and I love you, and I want us to bond."

Devon finally looked up. Lorcan was staring at him, probably trying to read him, and Devon didn't want him to. He wanted Lorcan to believe him and not try to find out what was happening.

They were both silent for a moment, then, to Devon's relief, Lorcan seemed to find what he was looking for in Devon's expression. He nodded, and Devon felt a weight lift from his shoulders.

He wouldn't have anything else, but this, he could have. He could be with Lorcan the way they were meant to be, at least for tonight.

Devon took his hands away from Lorcan's and reached up, hooking his hands around his mate's neck. He pulled, and Lorcan came closer. Devon suspected he was still hesitant about bonding, but it didn't look like he was about to stop Devon. Devon took advantage of that, kissing his mate and hoping it would be enough to distract Lorcan.

Then he found the same problem again—he couldn't open Lorcan's jeans. Lorcan didn't try to stop him this time, though. Instead, he chuckled and reached down, opening his jeans himself before turning his attention to Devon's. Devon was glad for that. He didn't think he'd be able to do any of this, not with the way his hands trembled.

"Why don't we get on the bed?" Lorcan murmured.

Devon nodded. He couldn't speak, not anymore. Instead he obeyed, taking his shoes off before sliding his now open jeans down his legs, then taking off his t-shirt. He shivered, but not because it was cold. He was trembling with anticipation, but it was also hard for him to stop thinking about the fact that this was the only occasion he'd have to be with Lorcan. He had to push away those thoughts, though. He should focus on Lorcan, not on a future he couldn't change.

He climbed onto the bed and turned around. The room was dark, but enough light came in from the window that he could see Lorcan's silhouette as he stripped. He wished he could see more, but he didn't want to ask. He wasn't sure he could do this with the light on, and Lorcan would no doubt realize something was up if he did ask. He could read Devon better than Devon could himself sometimes.

"I don't know what happened, but I won't ask you if you're sure again," Lorcan said as he followed Devon onto the bed.

"You're an adult, and you know your own mind. You have to let me know if anything I do makes you uncomfortable, though. You haven't told me what Elroy did to you exactly, and I don't want to—"

Devon kissed him again. He pressed himself closer to Lorcan, wanting him to focus on him rather than on what he'd been about to say. Lorcan meant well, but Devon wasn't going to freak out. He wanted this more than anything.

Lorcan was entirely bare. Devon found out when he plastered his body against his mate's. He almost jerked back in surprise, but he managed to keep himself under control. He wouldn't change his mind, and he had to stop behaving like a virginal teenager.

"What do you want?" Lorcan asked as he stroked up and down Devon's back. His fingertips dipped just under the elastic band of Devon's underwear, and Devon waited, holding his breath.

Lorcan's fingers moved lower until one of them slipped between Devon's ass cheeks.

"Too much?" Lorcan asked.

Devon shook his head. "I want you inside me." He was desperate for it.

Lorcan nodded and rolled away, leaving Devon cold. Instead of waiting for Lorcan to come back, Devon quickly pushed his underwear down his legs, dropping them to the floor. By the time he was done, Lorcan was back, and Devon opened his legs for him.

Lorcan didn't ask him if he was sure again. Instead, Devon heard the *snick* of a bottle of lube being opened. It was easy to focus on Lorcan after that. Devon was aware that every time he was touched, it was his mate touching him. Lorcan's touch was gentle but sure, and even though Devon's heart was racing and felt like it might explode at any second, he wasn't scared. He could feel Lorcan. He could smell him, even though he wasn't a shifter. His world was focused on his mate right now, and the fear faded away as Lorcan prepped him.

Just like for everything else when it came to Devon, Lorcan took his time to make sure he was ready for him and that he wouldn't hurt him. Devon was pretty sure there were four fingers inside of him, pushing in and sliding out, by the time Lorcan deemed him ready to take his cock.

Devon was relieved. He'd been writhing under Lorcan's touch, clutching the sheets under him and rolling his head on the pillow. He needed more. He needed Lorcan — Lorcan's cock in his body, Lorcan's blood coursing through him.

Lorcan was still taking his time, though, and Devon had enough. He grabbed Lorcan's arm, stopping him, then pulled him closer. Lorcan had to settle between Devon's legs for the position to be comfortable for the two of them, and his cock slipped between Devon's slick ass cheeks. Devon's breath hitched, but it wasn't enough, not yet.

"I love you," Lorcan whispered. "I've loved you since the first day I saw you, wary and diffident, and it's never going to change. I'll always love you. You're my mate, and I'll cherish you for the rest of your life."

Devon's eyes burned. "I know. I love you, too." But the rest of his life would be much shorter than Lorcan could imagine, and a sense of urgency clung to Devon. It was the reason why he tilted his hips up to give Lorcan easier access, the reason he reached between them to angle Lorcan's cock the right way. He took a moment to savor the instant, to feel Lorcan's cock and the weight of his body on him.

Then the head of Lorcan's cock pressed against Devon's hole, and Devon held his breath.

It was tight, and he could feel his body stretching to accommodate his mate. There was a pinch, radiating pain, but Lorcan had done a good job, and soon Devon was able to relax. He let the pleasure wash over him, and Lorcan guided his movements, pulling him down every time he thrust inside. The care Lorcan put into it made Devon sob, and he pressed his fist to his mouth, biting his knuckles. Lorcan would have none of that, though. He caught Devon's hand, pulled it away, and kissed his knuckles, then his cheek, his lips.

Devon gave in. It was easy. He tilted his head to the side and screwed his eyes shut as Lorcan's rhythm changed, became faster. Lorcan grunted, and Devon felt his warm breath against his neck. He tensed, but the pain was just a flash, brief like lightning.

Then there was only pleasure.

Devon felt Lorcan's mouth pull on the wound he'd created. He scrambled, needing to finish the bond, to be one with Lorcan, but like always, Lorcan seemed to know what he wanted. He let go of Devon's neck, and Devon whined, wanting him back. He got what he wanted only seconds later, and the scent of blood hit his nose. It wasn't his—it was Lorcan's, because Lorcan had cut his own neck so that Devon could drink his blood.

Devon latched onto the wound. He wrinkled his nose, but he was too far gone to care much about the taste of warm copper in his mouth. Lorcan was hammering inside him now, and it was hard to keep sucking when every thrust pushed Devon upward. He clung to Lorcan's shoulders as hard as he could, and he managed, at least until he felt the bond slide into place.

It felt like the most natural thing in the world, and Devon gave in to it, throwing his head back as he came. His release slicked their movements even more, and he held on until he felt Lorcan shudder against him. He could feel that Lorcan was coming, too, that he was filling him with his release. There would always be a part of Lorcan inside Devon now, just like Devon would always be part of Lorcan.

They were both panting, and it was hard for Devon to

breathe. Lorcan seemed to realize it, and after a moment, he rolled off. Devon moved with him, not wanting to let him go, not yet.

"We should clean up," Lorcan murmured. He stroked up and down Devon's back, making Devon feel like a cat.

He sighed. "We can wait. Try to sleep."

"You, too."

"Of course."

But Devon knew it was a lie. As soon as Lorcan was asleep, he would leave, and he'd never be back. He had to bite his lower lip hard so he wouldn't start sobbing. He'd thought he had everything, but Elroy was taking it away again, and Devon knew he wouldn't survive it.

Not this time.

CHAPTER SIX

Devon was gone when Lorcan woke up. For the first few seconds, he didn't think there was anything wrong with that. Then he remembered Devon would never go around on his own, not in the enforcers' building where a lot of people lived.

He frowned and sat up, looking at the bathroom door. Maybe Devon was in there, but the door was open, and no sounds came out of the room. Lorcan hesitated. He didn't want to freak out if there was no reason to. Maybe Devon really was downstairs. Maybe whatever had happened between them last night had made him see that he could truly trust the people in Lorcan's life. Still, that didn't feel right, and Lorcan reached for the bond, but he couldn't feel much, as if Devon were asleep.

That didn't make sense, either. He should be asleep next to Lorcan.

Maybe Devon had freaked out after they'd bonded and Lorcan had fallen asleep. Maybe he'd gone home, not thinking about how Lorcan would feel when he woke up and he wasn't there. Lorcan didn't like that though, but if that was what had happened, at least he knew Devon would be safe.

He didn't want to think about any other option right now.

He wanted to call Justin and ask him if he'd seen Devon, but he didn't want to freak Justin and Yedley out if there was no reason to. He decided to go downstairs first, praying he'd find Devon there, having breakfast and talking with his friends. The rest of Lorcan's team knew who Devon was and that they were mates, so if they saw him wandering the house, they would take him under their wings.

Lorcan quickly washed up, dressed, and went to the kitchen. Part of his team was there, sitting at the counter and eating breakfast. Jonathan looked up when he heard Lorcan, and his smile widened. "I heard you have a visitor last night," he teased.

Lorcan couldn't go along with it. He looked around the kitchen, but he wasn't surprised to see Devon wasn't there.

Devon wasn't in the *building*. Sometime last night after they'd made love, he'd left, and Lorcan had no idea where he was.

"Lorcan? Everything okay?" Jonathan asked, and Lorcan realized he was freaking his friend out by not answering.

"Have you seen Devon?" he asked.

Jonathan blinked. "No. We thought he was still with you." He looked at Tanner, who was sitting next to him. "Have you seen Devon?"

Tanner shook his head and swallowed his piece of bacon before answering. "No. We thought he was still with you. I mean, it made sense. He's kind of afraid of everyone except you, Justin, and Yedley."

"He wasn't there when I woke up, and I don't think he's anywhere in the house." Lorcan could feel the edge of panic in his voice, and he wanted it to stop. He didn't *want* to panic. He wanted to stay cool and make sure Devon was okay.

Jonathan rose from his chair. "How about you call Justin? It wouldn't be the first time Devon got spooked and left, would it?"

"He's done it before," Lorcan confirmed.

"Call Justin, then. Maybe we're worrying for nothing and Devon's home."

Lorcan wanted to believe that, but something was telling him that wasn't the case. Whatever had happened to Devon, wherever he was right now, it was bad. Still, Lorcan needed to be sure, so he took his phone out and dialed Justin's number. Justin answered after a few rings. "What's wrong?" he asked.

Lorcan blinked. "Why would you think something is wrong?"

"I don't know. I thought Devon—never mind. Do you need anything? How's Devon?"

The bottom of Lorcan's stomach dropped. If Justin was asking how Devon was, then he hadn't seen him today. "That's what I was calling about. I wanted to know if you'd seen him."

There was a pause, then Justin said, "I haven't. He asked Yedley to shimmer him to you last night."

"I know. He spent part of the night with me, but he wasn't there when I woke up this morning. Are you sure he hasn't come home during the night?"

"Let me check." Lorcan listened to the sounds of Justin going to Devon's bedroom. He heard Justin knock and ask Devon if he was in there, then the creak of the door opening. "The bed hasn't been slept in," Justin finally said.

Lorcan wasn't surprised. He'd expected precisely this, but it still hurt.

"Maybe he's somewhere else in the house," Justin continued, but both he and Lorcan knew that wasn't the case.

Lorcan tightened his hold around his phone. "Something happened to him," he said through gritted teeth.

"Don't freak out. We don't know if something did happen. I understand why it's the first thing you think of, but maybe he's in town or something? Maybe he needed to take a walk. I don't know what happened between the two of you, but—"

"We bonded. That's what happened, and he never would leave me like that after what we did. I *know* something happened to him."

There was a pause before Justin answered. "I agree with you. Even if he'd left you, if he'd gotten scared, he would have come home. This isn't like him. Did he say anything to you?"

"No. We had our date last night, and it went well. Then he popped up at my door about half an hour later, and he felt desperate." As if he'd been planning to do something. As if his time with Lorcan was coming to an end. Lorcan sucked in a breath. "You don't think Elroy got him, do you?"

"I don't know, Lorcan. Devon would never go to him of his own volition, not after what the man did to him, but maybe something happened. Do you know if Devon had anyone at all he could use as leverage to get him back?"

"He has a sister." It was the only person who came to mind, and Lorcan wouldn't be surprised if Elroy used her to get Devon to come back. Hell, now that he thought about it, he was almost a hundred percent sure that was what was happening.

Devon had found out Elroy had his sister, and he'd come to Lorcan to have one last night with him before he went back to Elroy. It had to be something like that, if not exactly that.

Lorcan almost threw his phone against the wall. He was angry, but not at Devon. He wanted to get his hands on Elroy and kill him, but he wouldn't, not without hurting him first. After everything the man had done, after the way he'd treated Devon, he deserved to be in as much pain as possible.

"Take a deep breath," Jonathan said, startling Lorcan, who hadn't realized Jonathan had come closer.

He took Lorcan's phone from his hand, and Lorcan was grateful. He didn't want to break it. He might need it if Devon called him.

But he knew his mate wouldn't. He was in Elroy's hands, and that wasn't going to change.

"Justin and Yedley are coming," Jonathan said as he hung up.

Lorcan nodded. He knew he couldn't go out there halfcocked. He had to breathe and find out exactly what had happened, where Devon and Elroy were, and what was going on. He couldn't rush this. He couldn't risk it, not when Devon's life was at stake.

But he didn't like feeling useless, especially knowing that Devon was probably getting hurt right now. He needed to do something, but what?

When Devon woke up, he was still handcuffed to the wall. He wasn't surprised. He'd known this would happen when he'd decided to come back. What *did* surprise him was that he still hadn't seen Elroy. He'd thought Elroy would be there waiting for him when he came back, but instead, he'd been met by guards. They hadn't been gentle with him, but they also hadn't hurt him, except when they'd handcuffed him to the wall.

And Devon wasn't alone. Cedric was there, too, hand-cuffed on the opposite wall. He was asleep, and Devon took a moment to look at him. He kept twitching, as if in pain, and Devon hated that he'd caused that. He should have thought better about what would happen to the people he left behind when he'd run away, but instead, he'd thought only about himself.

Cedric was bruised, and there was blood at the corner of his lips. Devon wondered if he could see anything, given how bad his eyes were swollen, but he wasn't about to wake Cedric up to check. If Cedric had managed to fall asleep, it meant he needed the rest, and Devon wasn't going to inter-rupt it.

He looked around. He didn't recognize the place where he and Cedric were being held, but then there wasn't much to recognize. The room was bare cement — gray everywhere, with no window. There was nothing in it, and the door was closed so Devon couldn't see out. The guards had covered his eyes after they'd caught him, so he had no idea where he'd ended up. They hadn't been far from Elroy's house, because they hadn't taken a car, walking instead. That was all Devon knew, though, and that didn't bode well if he wanted to make an escape.

He probably shouldn't.

Cedric had been hurt because Devon had left, and Devon could too easily imagine who would get hurt the next time. Himself, no doubt. Although he doubted Elroy would allow him out of his sight long enough for him to try to run away again. Now that he had Devon, he was going to make sure Devon wasn't going anywhere.

Devon's stomach churned with anxiousness and fear. He'd believed it was over. He'd thought he'd made it out, that he would finally be able to have a good life. Instead, he was here, and he was going to be tortured. He didn't know if Elroy would kill him, but he hoped he did. It would be better than anything else he could do to Devon.

Cedric groaned and tried to open his eyes, but Devon wasn't sure it was possible. "Stay still," he said, keeping his voice soft.

Cedric froze, listening. "Devon?" he asked.

"It's me. How are you feeling?"

"What are you doing here?"

"What did you think I was going to do when I found out he was torturing you? I came back. He promised he'd let you go if I did."

Cedric laughed, but it wasn't a happy sound. "And you think he's going to do it? Come on, Devon. You know him better than that. We both do."

He wasn't wrong. Devon would do everything he could to make sure Cedric made it out of here, but he already knew he couldn't count on Elroy's word. Elroy never kept it. "I'll find a way to get you out of here."

"There *is* no way. That's why you shouldn't have come back." Cedric sighed. "I should have gone with you the first time. Now we're both stuck here."

Devon looked around. There was nowhere for either of them to go, but Cedric was a shifter. He was a tiny shifter, too — a mouse. "Maybe you could shift," he said.

Cedric groaned. "Nothing has ever sounded so bad right now. Do you know how painful it's going to be?"

"I don't. But if it's the only way for you to get out, then you need to take it."

"Even if I shift, I can't leave this place. There's nowhere to go."

"The door's locked, but I'm sure we can get someone to open it."

"How?"

Devon bit his lower lip. "We'll tell the guard you have to go to the bathroom."

Cedric snorted, then jerked, maybe with pain. "And you think they're going to care? I'm already bloody and dirty and sweaty. What will it change if I pee myself?"

"The guards might not care, but Elroy will. Trust me. I know, and I suspect they do, too." For all that Elroy was a sadistic asshole, he didn't like offending smells or getting dirty. He wouldn't be happy with the state Cedric was in. Devon didn't know what Elroy was planning for Cedric, but if Cedric was still there when he arrived, he wouldn't like the stink. It was Cedric's only chance, and they had to take it.

"If you manage to get out of here, you have to go to Gillham," Devon said, his voice urgent. He needed Cedric to understand. He needed him to get to Gillham and to Lorcan. Maybe there was a way for them to make it out of this again. And if there wasn't, well, at least Devon would die knowing

Cedric was safe.

"Is that where you were? In Gillham?"

"It is." Devon hesitated. He wasn't sure that saying it out loud was a good idea, but he wanted Cedric to understand. "I ran there because I wanted to warn them about what Elroy was planning," he confessed. Cedric sucked in a breath, but he didn't say anything, so Devon continued, "I met people there. I lived with some of them until now, and they protected me. I also met my mate."

"Your mate?"

"Yes. I left him behind, but I know he'll protect you if you go there. Please, Cedric. I need to know you'll be okay. I need to know I didn't come back for nothing."

Cedric was silent, and Devon expected him to refuse. He had the first time, so it wouldn't be a surprise. "I can't believe you went to Gillham," Cedric finally said.

"Of course I went there. I needed to warn them. And I know they'll keep you safe. Just tell them you're my friend."

"Just like that?"

"Just like that. I promise." He could see Cedric wasn't convinced, but he nodded, and they put their plan in action.

Cedric started yelling that he needed to go to the bathroom, and for a bit, the guards didn't react. But after about ten minutes, one of them opened the door and glared at them. "Stop shouting," he snapped.

"He needs to go to the bathroom," Devon said. "And before you say no, you know Elroy won't like it if he pees himself in here."

The guard paused, then glared both at Devon and Cedric. Devon was relieved when the guard moved toward Cedric and unlocked the handcuffs that kept him tied to the wall. Devon and Cedric exchanged a glance, and Cedric nodded. He couldn't shift in here, just in case the guard managed to close the door again, but once he was outside, he was going to try. Hopefully, his animal form was small enough that he would manage to sneak away.

Devon didn't want to hope that having Cedric run away would help *him*, though. Elroy would be pissed when he finally arrived, and he would take it out on Devon, like always. But if the only thing that came out of it was that Cedric was safe, that would be okay with Devon. He wasn't looking forward to it, but it was better than knowing Cedric had died because of him.

The door closed behind Cedric and the guard, and Devon closed his eyes. He listened, and he heard the moment in which Cedric shifted and ran away. The guard started yelling, and someone ran just outside the door of Devon's cell.

Then, nothing. Devon had no idea whether Cedric had managed to run away, but he hoped so. He only opened his eyes when he heard someone walk closer. He recognized the footsteps, and he sucked in a breath.

This was it. Elroy had arrived, and Devon knew his day would end in pain.

The door opened, and Elroy stepped in. Devon tried to sit up, to face the man head-on. He was terrified, and he knew that whatever happened, he would lose, but he wouldn't go down like a coward. He'd already done enough of that.

Elroy was pissed. Devon recognized his expression, and he steeled himself for what was coming.

"Your little friend ran away," Elroy said. His voice was deceptively calm, but Devon knew better.

"I'm glad he did."

"Are you, pet? So would I be right if I said you helped him?"

Devon rattled the handcuffs. "I couldn't exactly help, could I? So, no. I had nothing to do with it, but I'm still glad he left. I would if I could."

"You came back to me."

"Only because you tortured my friend. I wouldn't be here otherwise."

Elroy moved closer, and Devon couldn't help but shrink against the wall. He felt fingers slide over his cheekbones, and he shuddered in disgust. He didn't want this. The only person he wanted to touch him that way was Lorcan, but he was far away in Gillham.

Elroy caught Devon's chin, and with a painful grip, forced him to look at him. Devon knew it would leave finger-shaped bruises.

It always did.

"You were an idiot," Elroy said. "You should have known better than to run away from me. I told you I would always find you, and I did."

Devon didn't say anything. What *could* he say? Besides, his jaw hurt, and Elroy was still holding it. He knew what he was doing to Devon, and he took pleasure in it. Devon's eyes burned from the pain Elroy was inflicting and because he knew he would never see Lorcan and his friends again. He wanted nothing more than to go back to Gillham, but he knew that part of his life was over. Whatever remained of it would be spent with Elroy, and with pain.

Elroy's eyes widened, then he narrowed them. He used his hold on Devon's chin to tilt his head to the side, and Devon knew what he'd seen. "Who did that?" Elroy asked, barely contained fury in his voice.

"My mate." Devon licked his lips. "He's ten times the man you can ever be. I let him fuck me and claim me, and that is something you will never have. I know we were never mates, Elroy. I hate you for almost taking this away from me, but you didn't in the end. I got it, and I was happy."

"*Was*, Devon. You're not with your mate anymore, and honestly, I don't care that you know you're not mine. It won't change anything." He paused, then skimmed a fingertip on the bite. Devon never wanted him to touch it, but he couldn't go anywhere. He couldn't move, not when Elroy was holding him still. "Besides, I can still try to bite you right over the scar. It won't be the same thing, but it will reclaim you as mine. I might even do it while I'm fucking you. I'm going to take away all the signs your mate left on you, and you'll be mine again."

Devon closed his eyes. It was exactly what he'd feared, and now, he was going to have to live through it.

When Justin and Yedley arrived, Lorcan was on them in a second. He grabbed Yedley by the shoulders, forcing him to look at him. "You need to shimmer me to him," he said.

Justin growled and grabbed Lorcan, pulling him away from his mate. "Leave him alone," he snapped.

Lorcan's first instinct was to tell Justin to fuck off, but he couldn't. Justin was his friend, and more importantly, he was Devon's friend. He wanted to find Devon as much has Lorcan did, and fighting with him wouldn't help.

Lorcan sucked in a breath and rubbed his face. "I'm sorry," he said.

Yedley patted his shoulder. "Don't worry about it. I understand, and I want him back as much as you do. We can't go in there without knowing what's happening, though. I'm not an enforcer, and I don't want to put anyone at risk, least of all Devon."

He was right. He was here because he was Devon's friend, but he wasn't an enforcer. He didn't know how to deal with these things. Lorcan did, but he was panicking. Even *he* could admit that. Panic and fear were the worse things to feel on a mission. They caused mistakes, and in this case, mistakes couldn't be allowed, not when Devon's life was on the line.

"Breathe," Justin ordered. He wasn't the team leader, but

Lorcan obeyed anyway. He knew he had to. They were going to get Devon back, but they needed to do this the right way. It was hard to think, though. Lorcan had to close his eyes, and when he did, he forced himself to breathe once, then twice, then again. By the time he was calmer, the rest of his team had arrived, and so had Bran and Kameron.

They were standing around, looking at each other. Devon cleared his throat to explain what had happened. "He came here last night," he said. "We bonded. When I woke up, he was gone."

"How do you know he went back to Elroy?" Bran asked. "Because we all know what Elroy did to him. Why would he go back?"

"Nothing else makes sense, though. He didn't have a reason to run." Lorcan narrowed his eyes. "I didn't force him to bond with me, if that's what you're thinking."

Bran shook his head. "Of course not. I know you wouldn't do anything like that. Maybe he panicked. Maybe he's just hiding out somewhere, and he'll come back."

"I think Lorcan is right," Justin said. "If Devon had panicked, he would have come back home. It's his safe place. The fact that he's nowhere to be found and that he won't answer his phone is worrying. I wouldn't be surprised if Elroy had managed to find him. We can't dismiss that possibility, even though I know it's not what we want."

Bran sighed and nodded. "You're right. You know him better than I do, so I'm going to trust you on this. We need to work with the assumption that Elroy has him, then. Does anyone know where he could be? Can we find him and shimmer to him?"

The team got together, and Lorcan tried to focus on what they were saying, but he couldn't. In this case, he wasn't behaving like an enforcer. He was behaving like a mate, like someone who was afraid he'd lost the best part of his life. The only thing he could think about was Devon being hurt. He could feel Devon in the back of his mind, and while there had been some pain, mostly there was fear. It made Lorcan's mouth taste like metal, and he didn't know if he would ever be able to get rid of that taste.

He leaned against the wall and closed his eyes. He needed to stop focusing on the bond. It gave him a link to Devon, which was what he desperately wanted right now, but it wasn't helping. It was distracting him, and Devon needed him to be focused. It was the only way for him to find Devon and bring him home, which was what he was planning to do.

"How are you doing?" Jonathan asked.

Lorcan opened his eyes. "How do you think I'm doing?"

Jonathan grimaced. "I know. And trust me, if you decide just to run in there, I'll be right behind you, and so will the rest of us. We'll always be there for you. You know that."

"But this is the best way to do it. *I* know *that*."

"We'll get him back."

"Lorcan?" Bran asked.

Lorcan turned his attention to the head enforcer. "Yes?"

"You said you bonded with Devon?"

"We did. Last night."

"Can you feel him, then?"

Lorcan blinked. He hadn't realized what that meant. "I can."

"Yes?" Bran's smile was triumphant. "Then Elroy isn't as careful as we expected him to be. Maybe he didn't realize Devon had bonded. He probably doesn't even know Devon has friends now. Devon was alone when he arrived. I wouldn't be surprised if Elroy thought that was still the case. That means we have a chance to get him back."

They could shimmer to Devon. Elroy might be using a Nix blocker, but they would still be able to get close enough to get to Devon. They would no doubt have a fight on their hands,

114

but they could do this.

It was the best idea they could come up with. Elroy thought Devon was alone, but he wasn't, and eventually, Elroy would realize that. Then he would act, and they needed to be ahead of him. They had to get to Devon before Elroy closed their path to him.

Lorcan swallowed. "We have to move fast," he said.

Bran nodded. "I agree. We'll get your mate back, Lorcan. Don't worry about that."

"But we don't know what we're going up against," Sue said. She was the leader of Lorcan's team, and Lorcan respected her. Still, right now, he wished she hadn't spoken.

"We don't, but it's a risk we have to take. We don't leave anyone behind, least of all a mate," Bran said.

Sue nodded. "I know. It's not what I was suggesting. But maybe we could use this chance to do something about Elroy before he attacks Gillham."

Bran paused, and Lorcan could almost see the cogs turning in his brain. He was surprised when the man shook his head, though. "We'll get in and out with Devon. No matter how much I want to take this opportunity to do more damage and possibly get rid of Elroy, this isn't about him. It's about Devon. We know Elroy is working with the Beasts, and he might have a whole bunch of them, both there and around the country. They could still attack Gillham after we're done with him. We can't risk that. Right now, we know what Elroy is planning. We won't have that if he dies and someone else takes his place. We can't risk it. Besides, we still have people undercover. I trust they'll find out what's going on."

Lorcan was relieved. He understood what Sue was saying, and he was the first who wanted to get rid of Elroy. They had to think about Gillham and the pack, though. They had to think about the people they were protecting.

Bran looked at Lorcan. "Can you do this? No one will

blame you if you decide to stay here. We all understand how distracted you are."

Lorcan shook his head. "I have to come."

"I understand that. I'll leave the decision to your team leader, but I think you shouldn't be in the first wave. Stay behind. Let the others fight whoever is there while you look for Devon. Focus on him."

Bran didn't have to say that for Lorcan to know. He might want to tear Elroy and his people apart with his bare hands, but now wasn't the time. Now was the time to focus on Devon and save him, and that was what Lorcan would do.

He couldn't have done anything else even if he'd wanted to, and he didn't.

Every single inch of Devon's body hurt. He was curled on the cold, hard floor, trying to protect what he could, especially his face. Elroy didn't usually hit him there because he liked to keep him pretty, as he said, but today, he seemed to be especially angry. It was because of the mark Lorcan had left on his shoulder, but not just that. Devon had never talked back to Elroy the way he had today. He'd never dared.

But now he knew there was more to life than Elroy. He knew Elroy was a liar, an abuser, and that he didn't deserve anything Devon could give him. Devon certainly wasn't going to give him respect. Elroy already had his fear, but Devon was managing it, to his own surprise.

The pain was a different problem, though.

Elroy had beaten Devon, which was better than what Devon had expected. Devon had thought Elroy would rape and bite him, and he'd been petrified at the thought. He didn't want Elroy to take the bond away from him. He didn't know if it was possible, but he didn't want to risk it. That was one of the reasons he'd kept on provoking Elroy until Elroy had snapped and started beating him.

"You made me angry, pet," Elroy drawled. He was panting, something that didn't surprise Devon, considering how hard he'd been beating him.

Devon was pretty sure he had at least a few broken bones, if not more, and it was getting hard to breathe. It could be because of the panic, but Devon couldn't tell for sure, and it was worrying. He felt like he was about to die, and he didn't want that to happen.

"You let someone else touch what was mine," Elroy continued. He dug his fingers into Devon's hair and pulled Devon's head back. It was painful, but it was almost imperceptible next to everything else. Still, Devon winced, and when Elroy shook him, he knew he had to open his eyes and look at him. It was what Elroy expected, and Devon gave in. He wasn't sure he could stand any more pain.

Elroy was staring at him. He looked like he'd run a marathon—red, sweaty, and agitated. It told Devon it wasn't over, not by a longshot. Elroy made a disgusted sound and pushed Devon back to the ground. "Of course you made me angry. It's what you're best at. But you're mine, Devon, and you always will be."

Devon was tempted to tell him to go fuck himself. He wanted Elroy to know that he'd never been his, and he never would be. He didn't think he could stand another beating right now, though, so he kept his mouth shut. He would have time to mouth off at Elroy the next time Elroy decided to beat him up.

Because it would happen—Elroy had made it clear. He was going to make Devon pay for what he'd done, and that payment always came in pain. It was what Elroy was good at, and Devon had been aware of it when he'd decided to come back.

He still didn't regret it. No matter how much it hurt, no matter what Elroy had planned for him, at least Cedric was free. He'd run away, and Devon knew he wouldn't come back. Even if he wanted to help Devon, he knew better. Coming back would mean death, probably for both of them.

It would be preferable to being with Elroy. It was easy to imagine what Elroy would do to Devon if he kept him around, and Devon decided that if Elroy's beatings didn't kill him, he would take care of that himself. He wasn't afraid of death. It would be better than going through this day and after day.

"You forced my hand, pet. Not only did you run away, but you allowed another man to fuck you, and when you came back, you mouthed off at me. You deserve this. I'm glad you found a little backbone, but you need to stop. We both know you're weak and that you're behaving this way is because you're mad at me. Just remember. The only reason I'm hurting you is because of what you did."

Devon almost snorted. He wasn't surprised Elroy was blaming him. It was what he always did. If he hurt Devon, it was Devon's fault. Never Elroy's.

Desperation was gripping at Devon's stomach. He needed to get out of here, but he wasn't even sure he could move. Maybe this was the right moment to provoke Elroy, to push him to the brink and have him kill him. It was all Devon could think about, and he opened his mouth to do just that, but a wave of love came through the bond, reminding him that he wasn't alone anymore.

He wanted to die. He wanted to go home. Lorcan was aware that Devon was gone, and Devon had no doubt he was going to try to come for him. He might be too late, or he might not arrive at all. Devon wouldn't be surprised. He had no idea where he was, but Elroy was smart. That was one of the reasons the council hadn't managed to find him yet.

Lorcan would try, and he wouldn't be the only one. There was still a chance for Devon to make it out of this alive, and even though the hope of that happening was small, Devon couldn't help but grasp at it.

If there was one person who could find and save him, it was Lorcan.

Devon swallowed, tasting blood — his own blood this time.

No matter how much he wanted Lorcan to come, he needed his mate to stay away. This wouldn't end well. If Lorcan was alone, well, he would probably be captured and hurt, if not killed. If there was someone with him, they might have a chance to get to Devon, but it would make Elroy even angrier than he already was. He might realize that Devon had been staying in Gillham, and he would strike. Devon didn't know if Gillham was ready for that to happen. They knew it was coming, but they were still getting ready, preparing the people who lived there, gathering even more enforcers. Devon had given them time, but it would be for nothing if they forced Elroy's hand.

Devon shouldn't have bonded with Lorcan. Just the thought of not doing it made him want to throw up, but he couldn't deny it. If he hadn't bonded with his mate, Lorcan wouldn't have been able to feel him. He wouldn't know what was happening, and he wouldn't be trying to get to him. He might have thought Devon had decided it was too much for him and that he'd left. Instead, he knew what Devon was going through, and that enraged Devon. He didn't want Lorcan to feel his pain. He didn't want Lorcan to put himself in danger. He wanted Lorcan to be happy, to live his life and find someone else.

He'd messed this up, too, and he wasn't surprised. He'd been selfish, focusing on what he wanted. When he'd realized he was going back to Elroy, he'd wanted one last chance to be happy. And he had been. He'd felt cherished, and it was all thanks to Lorcan. But now, that feeling was putting Lorcan and everyone else he was bringing with him in danger. It had been a moment of weakness, and Devon was terrified that someone else was going to pay for it.

Elroy poked him with the tip of his shoe, and Devon groaned in pain. "You're worthless," Elroy said. "You can't even stand a little pain. I guess I should give you some time to recover before I come back."

He smiled, and Devon knew what would happen the next time. Elroy had been angry today, which was why he'd beaten Devon without trying to do anything more. Devon wouldn't be as lucky when Elroy came back, though.

Elroy kicked him in the back again, then moved away. Devon tried to breathe through the pain. He watched Elroy leave the room, and only then did he allow himself to cry.

He'd ruined everything. He should have stayed with Elroy from the beginning. He shouldn't have told Lorcan he wanted to bond. He shouldn't have allowed Lorcan in his life. It wouldn't have hurt so much if he hadn't.

"What did he do to you?" someone close to Devon said.

Devon jerked back. He hit the wall, and he cried out, pain filling his body and making it feel like it was on fire. Someone crouched in front of him, and he forced himself to open his eyes. For a moment, he couldn't believe what he was seeing. He thought he was hallucinating, which wouldn't be surprising with all the blows he'd taken to the head.

But it really was Lorcan. He was there, in front of Devon, reaching for him but not touching him, maybe afraid he would hurt him. A woman stood behind him, and she was staring at the door, her expression fierce.

Lorcan swallowed audibly, then touched the top of Devon's head, which surprisingly, was one of the few spots that didn't hurt. He held his other hand back, and the woman took it.

"Take us away. He needs a doctor," Lorcan said.

"You can't stay here. He's going to kill you if he finds you,"

Devon croaked.

Lorcan shook his head. His smile was sad, but he *was* smiling. "Don't worry about Elroy. We're taking you home."

Devon closed his eyes. He didn't know if Lorcan was really present or if he'd taken too many blows to the head, but whichever the case, he wanted to live in this moment just for a few more seconds.

CHAPTER SEVEN

Lorcan wanted to take Devon's hand, but he wasn't sure he should. He didn't know if it would hurt as much as the rest of Devon's body no doubt did.

Devon had been unconscious by the time they'd shimmered back to pack territory. They'd gone straight to the infirmary, and Dallas had pushed Lorcan away, ordering him to keep his distance while he helped Devon. Even though Lorcan trusted him and the people he worked with, it had been hard. He'd wanted to stick with Devon, so he hadn't left the infirmary, but seeing his mate bloody and bruised was hell. It had made Lorcan want to go straight back to Elroy and beat his ass up, but thankfully, Jonathan and Tanner had been there, and they'd managed to distract him. Now they were gone, as were Dallas and Sei, the Nix who worked with him.

They'd left Devon and Lorcan alone, but Devon hadn't woken up yet. Dallas had been reassuring, telling Lorcan that the only reason he hadn't was that he was sleeping. His body would need a lot of rest to heal, even with Sei's ministrations. Devon was human, and even though he was the strongest person Lorcan had ever known, it meant his healing would be slower than a shifter's. Thankfully, Sei was there, and he would heal Devon a little more every day. It would still take time, and it would be painful, but Lorcan wasn't planning on going anywhere. He was staying here with Devon until Devon was ready to leave the infirmary.

He was sitting next to Devon's bed right now, and he wanted to touch him. He wanted to reassure himself and his eagle that their mate was okay. He could see it with his eyes, and he could feel it through the bond, but he needed more.

He'd been terrified when they'd shimmered into the room and he'd found Devon against the wall, curled into a tight, bloody ball. He'd been afraid Devon was already dead, and he wouldn't have been surprised, considering the state he'd been in. But Elroy hadn't been finished with him, which made Lorcan's stomach churn. Elroy had been planning to hurt Devon even more, and that was the only reason he'd left Devon in that room. His cruelty had given Devon a chance to escape, though.

Devon groaned. Lorcan jerked and leaned closer, his hand hovering over Devon's on the sheet. Instead of taking it, he stroked his fingertips on the back of it, hoping it was enough for Devon to know he wasn't alone.

Devon opened his eyes, and Lorcan could have cried. Instead, he moved closer so that Devon could see him. "Don't try to move. I know you're in a lot of pain, and I can call the doctor if you need me to," he said.

Of course, Devon didn't obey. Instead of staying still, he tried to sit up. Lorcan had to touch him this time, if anything to make sure he wasn't going to hurt himself even more. He gently pushed on Devon's chest, hoping it would be enough to keep him on the bed. "I said not to move," he repeated.

Devon shook his head. "What did you do?" he asked, breathless.

Lorcan blinked. "Nothing. What are you talking about?"

"You don't understand. This is one more reason for Elroy to attack. He promised me he wouldn't attack if I came back. He promised he'd let Cedric go. But now he doesn't have a reason to do any of that. He's going to attack, and it's going to be my fault." The panic in Devon's voice rose, and Lorcan was at a loss.

"You need to calm down," he said, his voice a bit harsher

than before.

Devon seemed to understand that better, and he stopped trying to sit up. His eyes were wide and damp, and he stared at Lorcan, waiting.

Lorcan cleared his throat. "I don't care what he promised he would or wouldn't do, Devon. He's a liar. He's an asshole, and the only reason he said that was that he wanted you back. You really think he wouldn't have attacked once he had you?"

Devon sucked in a breath. "I know. But I had to try."

"I know." Lorcan didn't like it, but he did understand. "You were trying to do what was best for Gillham, for the people who took you in and helped you. And it's a nice thing, but trust me, having you back here won't change anything. Elroy never planned to keep his promises. Did he let your friend go?"

Devon shook his head, wincing at the improvement. "He didn't. Cedric ran away. He was wounded. Did you find him?"

"You were alone in the room."

"He's a mouse shifter. I told him to run, and he did."

"I hope he's okay, but we can't go back to make sure. I'm sorry."

Devon closed his eyes, and a lone tear fell from one of them. Lorcan reached out and touched it, drying it. When he leaned back, Devon was looking at him again.

Lorcan forced himself to smile. It was almost impossible when he saw his mate in this much pain, but he wanted to bring a bit of normalcy in Devon's life. "I know you're in pain. I'm not going anywhere until you feel better. And when Elroy comes, we'll fight him together. You're not alone anymore. You have me, but not just me. You have Justin and Yedley and my team. You have the entire pack. You scared all of us when you disappeared, and even though I understand why you did it, I need you to promise me you won't do it again. I don't care what Elroy says. He's never going to keep any of his promises. I don't think I could stand seeing you in this state again, Devon. Please. I'm begging you. If anything like this happens again, you have to come to me or to someone else. If you don't trust me, that's fine. Talk to Justin, or Yedley, or even Kameron or Bran."

"Of course I trust you," Devon murmured.

Lorcan knew lack of trust wasn't the reason Devon hadn't talked to him before leaving. He'd known that Lorcan would try to stop him, and he'd thought he was doing the right thing. He'd thought he was doing the only thing possible.

"I love you," Devon continued. "I wouldn't have left if I didn't. I thought I was saving you and Gillham."

Lorcan's eyes burned, but he didn't want Devon to see how much pain he was in. His mate already had enough to deal with. "I love you too. I'm not going to let you sacrifice yourself, though."

"I don't think it would work a second time," Devon admitted.

A knock on the door made both of them glance up. Dallas had said Devon wouldn't be bothered, but Lorcan wasn't surprised someone was checking in on him. He looked at Devon, who nodded, then called out, "Come in."

The door opened, and Kameron stepped in. His expression hardened for a second when he saw the state Devon was in, but then he smiled. "Devon. I just wanted to check in on you," he said.

Devon tried to sit up again, but one glare from Lorcan sent him back to the mattress. "I've been better," he said.

Kameron smiled. "I'm sure you have. I couldn't help but hear what Lorcan was telling you before. I was in the hallway talking to Dallas, and you two weren't exactly quiet."

Lorcan hadn't realized they'd been so loud, but he didn't care. Whatever Kameron was trying to say, Devon probably needed to hear it.

"I'm sorry," Devon started.

"You have nothing to be sorry about. I know you were trying to help the town and the pack, and I'm grateful for that, but you didn't have to do it. Like Lorcan said, when we face Elroy, we'll do it together. You're not alone anymore, and if you want, you can be a pack member."

Devon blinked. "I'm not a shifter."

"That doesn't matter. Lorcan and his parents are pack members, even though they live in town. You can be one, too. Technically, you already are one. You're Lorcan's mate, and that's enough."

"I'm a Gillham pack member?" Devon asked, his voice trembling.

Kameron stepped closer and touched Devon's foot through the blanket. "You are. You have a family now, Devon, and we'll face whatever the future has for us together."

Lorcan couldn't have said it better. He hoped Devon wouldn't run away again, but if he did, Lorcan would go after him. He couldn't allow anyone to hurt his mate.

And once he got to Elroy, he would make sure the man paid. He'd hurt Devon, and he was planning to hurt the pack and the town. Lorcan was an enforcer, and protecting his people was his job.

He would do exactly that.

You may also enjoy the following from eXtasy Books Inc:

Stubborn Fangs
Catherine Lievens

Excerpt

Andrew found Aubrey just as Aubrey sat on the couch after spending most of the day guarding the coven. He groaned when he saw Andrew's face. He could tell from his friend's expression he wouldn't like whatever Andrew was about to ask.

He closed his eyes and tried to ignore Andrew, but Andrew stood there until Aubrey looked at him again. "What you want?" Aubrey asked.

"Falkner wants to visit Darren."

Aubrey groaned again. "Why? The man was planning on killing him. Why would he want to see him or be his friend?"

Andrew shrugged. "I have no idea, but I won't try to change him. He's a good man, and he acts like it."

"If you ask me, he should be less of a good man and think of his safety more."

"You know he won't do that. Anyway, he needs someone to go with him."

Aubrey had been right—he didn't like what he was

hearing. "Why don't you go with him?"

"I have something to do. I would if I could, but I can't."

"What about Richie?" Those three were together. Surely Richie could go with one of the men he loved?

Andrew shook his head. "He's working with James. He tried to get out of it, but you know he doesn't like it."

Because James needed to be able to control his shift and his werewolf. An out-of-control werewolf was never a pleasant thing to have on your hands, but especially so in a vampire coven.

Aubrey sighed. "Can he go later once one of you is back? I just sat down."

Andrew's expression was apologetic. "I know. I would ask someone else, but I trust you with his safety."

Aubrey knew Andrew wasn't doing it on purpose, but he was saying the exact things that would get Aubrey to get his ass off the couch and go with Falkner. He liked that Andrew trusted him with one of the men he loved. Most of the coven trusted him but Andrew and Falkner had been Aubrey's friends since they'd arrived. He wasn't their best friends — they'd been each other's best friend for so long that he wasn't sure anyone could change that, or at least, he hadn't been sure until Richie had arrived — but he was close to them, and he wanted them to be safe and happy.

He dropped the back of his head against the couch and closed his eyes again. "Fine. I'll go with him. I still think he's nuts, though."

"You and me both. I understand why he's doing this. He feels close to Darren because they're both dhampirs. I still don't like it, though."

That still stunned Aubrey. He wouldn't have known since when he'd met Falkner, Falkner had already been a vampire. It changed nothing for him, but he knew a few coven members had grumbled about Fyfe allowing Falkner to stay with them. Personally, he didn't care. He wouldn't have cared even if Falkner was a purple cow shifter. Falkner was Falkner, and

Aubrey loved him for who he was, not what he was. Besides, they already had two werewolves living with them. What did it change if a dhampir lived there, too? And there was Adrian. Aubrey loved him, even though he had no idea what to do with him most of the time, and even though Adrian was a vampire-werewolf hybrid. For whatever reason, Ignatius and Oscar had decided Aubrey was the perfect babysitter for their adopted son, and he couldn't get out of it, no matter how much he wanted to.

Maybe that was because he didn't actually want to. He might not know what to do with the baby, but he loved that kid.

He rose from the couch and stretched. "Where is he?"

Andrew looked relieved. "Still upstairs. I'll tell him you're waiting for him. I'll also tell him not to spend too much time there. I know you need some rest, and I'm really sorry I'm asking you to do this."

"But if you weren't asking me, he would go alone, and we both know that's a bad idea." Bad was an understatement.

Andrew looked away, clearly embarrassed. "I know I shouldn't be doing this. He's an adult, and he can protect himself."

"But he's just been attacked by a bunch of dhampirs, and you can't shake that fear. I get it. You don't have to explain, and I'm more than happy to go." Aubrey paused. "Well, I would have been more than happy if I hadn't just spent an entire day guarding the coven, but I can live with it." Besides, maybe Aubrey would be lucky enough to see Oren.

Ignatius worked for the conclave, and Oren was his team leader. That man was so hot that Aubrey hadn't been able to stop thinking about him, and he would always be grateful to James for being accused of murder and having Oren and his team come after him.

He doubted James felt the same way, though.

He was suspected Oren didn't like him, but that didn't matter, at least not much. It wasn't like they were getting married or anything. Aubrey just liked having some eye candy to look at while Falkner was busy with his murderous friend, and Oren was more like eye caviar or champagne, as far as he was concerned. He was delicious to look at, and Aubrey couldn't do it without wanting to lick him from head to toe.

He should probably stop thinking about that kind of stuff when he was with Oren, though. He was pretty sure every single thought showed in his expression, which would explain why Oren always looked like he'd rather be eating nails than spend any length of time with him.

Andrew patted Aubrey's shoulder. "Thanks. I'll tell him to come downstairs."

"And I'll be waiting." Unfortunately.

Since he had a little time, Aubrey headed to the downstairs bathroom. He washed his face and made sure his hair looked okay. He didn't know if Oren would be there, but since Ignatius was in the house and not out on a mission, there was a good chance he would be. He wouldn't be happy to see Aubrey—he never was—but Aubrey was convinced there was more to the distaste Oran seemed to have of him.

He didn't mind that Oren wasn't crazy about him. He might want to have sex with Oren, but he could take no for an answer, and he could limit himself to watching the guy. It was a pity, but Oren wasn't the first guy who didn't want Aubrey that way, and Aubrey could deal with it. He had plenty of times.

"Thanks for doing this," Falkner said when Aubrey walked into the entrance. He was already there, and he was bouncing on the balls of his feet.

Aubrey rolled his eyes. "You know Andrew asked me?"

"I do. I told him I could go alone, but he won't let me out of his sight if I'm on my own. I think it's ridiculous, but if it makes him feel better, who am I to say no?"

This was the kind of relationship Aubrey wanted. Falkner was fine on his own, but he understood that Andrew was worried, and he didn't mind doing this for him. It was a minor thing, a small gesture that showed how much Falkner cared for Andrew. Aubrey wanted the same, whether it was with Oren or someone else. He honestly didn't care. He wasn't in love with anyone at this point, although he couldn't deny he had a crush on Oren. But he knew nothing would come out of it, and that was fine. But as it was, he'd been single for a while, and he felt like he would never get laid again.

He huffed at his thoughts and turned his attention back to Falkner. "Let's go," he said.

Aubrey almost turned the car around only five minutes away from the house because Falkner opened his mouth and asked, "Are you hoping to see Oren?"

Aubrey had done his best to hide his crush. He didn't want Oren to be embarrassed, and he didn't want people to tease him. "I'm sorry?" he asked, keeping his gaze on the road.

"You don't have to hide it, not from me. I won't make fun of you. There's nothing to make fun of. I was just trying to make conversation and to check in on my friend."

Aubrey sighed. "Fine. I might have a little crush on him. It doesn't mean anything, though."

Falkner was widely smiling when Aubrey glanced at him. "It might not mean anything, but maybe it could."

"No. He's made it clear that he's irritated by me, and that he doesn't want to sleep with me."

"Did you ask him?"

"No." Aubrey could too easily imagine how that conversation would go. Oren would probably die of laughter or something.

"You can't know for sure, then. Why don't you give him a chance?"

"Because I'm pretty sure he would have made his move if he wanted anything more with me."

"Again, you can't know that. How could you? How many times have you spoken to him?"

"Not many," Aubrey had to admit. "Not because I didn't

want to. I've asked him out a few times, but he always said no." And Aubrey had stopped. He could see when he wasn't wanted.

"Maybe it wasn't that he didn't want to, but rather, that he was busy, or that he thinks he needs to focus on the job. A lot has been happening around town recently, and Oren's team is right in the middle of it. Why don't you try talking to him again? It might not get to anything, but if it does, you'll be happy."

Aubrey wasn't looking forward to being rejected once again, but maybe Falkner wasn't wrong. Maybe he needed to talk to Oren when things were a bit calmer, when he could have a nice conversation with the man instead of a quick chat in a hallway.

Aubrey didn't know, but knowing he had an option made him look at this visit with a smile. He still didn't understand why Falkner wanted to talk to Darren, but that didn't matter because Aubrey was going to talk to Oren.

About the Author

Catherine is the creator of several series, most of them paranormal, including the Whitedell Pride Series and the Gillham Pack Series. While she graduated in translation, she decided to go the writer's way because it was more fun to create her own stories and characters.

She's been living in Italy for more than twenty years, but she's a daughter of the North—Belgium to be precise—and she misses it so much that she's already planning to move back.

She loves pizza—probably too much—her son, her pets, and of course, books. She sneaks some reading time into her schedule every time she has five minutes free from writing, demands from her various pets and son, and lastly, housework.

Connect with her:

lievens.catherine@gmail.com
BookBub: https://www.bookbub.com/authors/catherine-lievens
Website: https://authorcatherinelievens.com/
Facebook: https://www.facebook.com/catherine.lievens.9
Facebook Group: https://www.facebook.com/groups/411788002341528/
Twitter: https://twitter.com/authorCLievens
Newsletter: http://eepurl.com/c-uvKn

www.ingramcontent.com/pod-product-compliance
Lightning Source LLC
Chambersburg PA
CBHW060623130626
46555CB00002B/629